THE LOTTERY MUST GO ON

"And it must fall on its tubes," she explained. Chet laughed. It didn't feel like a happy laugh.

"Do you know what'll happen to me if I purposely louse up your husband's lottery?"

With a quick nod, she raised an imaginary laserod, closed one eye to aim, and pulled the trigger. An imaginary beam hit him in the vulnerable spot that was her target. And it hurt. With her on the firing squad, he thought, a guy would have to let out the hem on his bulletproof vest.

SunStop 8

LOU FISHER

A DELL BOOK

To Paul Neimark

Published by
Dell Publishing Co., Inc.
1 Dag Hammarskjold Plaza
New York, New York 10017

ISBN: 0-440-12662-2

Printed in the United States of America
First printing—January 1978

SunStop 8

SUNSTOP 8
Chet McCoy
LOTTERY

Contents

Prologue

TOWERS

The following ad was apparently paid for from the combined funds of the AmDrive Fleet and Towers, Itpl. The microdot in the upper left margin indicates that the ad appeared in the York-Hudson NewsTapes during the year 2074.5.

THE SUNSTOPS!

EIGHT UNFORGETTABLE PLANETS
EVERYTHING UNDER TWO SUNS

•

All right. We admit it.

We're still not going to SunStop 8 for political reasons. And SunStop 1 is really too hot.

But the six in between are the miracles of the galaxy.

A multiparadise. A chain of tiny wonder-planets looping around a pair of flamboyant suns. Offering perpetually perfect weather, long beautiful days, crystal blue skies and waters, megameters of *natural* beaches . . . And there's more!

The Towers, awesome, the only hotel of its kind. Same for the exciting and health-giving SaunArena. And holoshows, lightball courts, crater skiing . . . Everything!

Find out more. Touch 32-0457 on your terminal.

It'll give you a good idea of just how much you can enjoy life. And just how much you can live.

Part One

CHET McCOY GOES FROM STOP TO STOP . . . AND ROCKY TAKES A LOOK

BELMONT
SHIFFMAN 77

1.
The Vice & McCoy Squad

The redhead seemed to be up for grabs.

Chet McCoy tried to reach her as she floated by, but his arms fell short of their goal, and she was gone again.

Frustrated, he kicked the pair of orange weights down toward his feet, letting the momentum swing him into a new trajectory. Now, gloriously, she was again in his sight. The silvon du-suit she wore gave him no view of soft flesh, but it outlined, roundly, a flying figure of tall and haughty proportions, more sleek than the AmDrive ship that had brought him to this wonderplanet. And, unlike the ship, she was a structure you wanted to get into. Not out of.

Doubling over with a grunt, he grabbed the weights from his legs and straightened, throwing them forward, hanging on as they pulled at his shoulders. He was carried directly toward her, and he was glad of that. *Because this goddamn gravless sauna,* he told himself, *is going to drive me crazy!*

"Hey," he called across the mist of the arena. "Why don't you aim yourself a little this way?" His voice sounded tired; he tried to make it louder. "We've been playing this game for a long time."

From the way she tossed the weights around, she'd started playing the game long before tonight. Suddenly, she was whipping across in front of him. For a brief moment he caught her curious stare. Perhaps, he thought, her eyes were always like that: a strange and penetrating blend of green hazes that asked a lot of questions but gave out no secrets of their own. The brief moment ended; she was quickly out of range, way off to his right. But the few words she left behind seemed to hang as hot and thick as the air around him.

"Who the hell are you?" was what she had said.

If it wasn't the sweetest tone of voice, it was at least better than the silence that had preceded it; and somehow it spurred him into hauling up his weights and flinging them out again, angled to throw him in her new and latest direction.

She switched again.

Another direction. A different level. Coming closer, then spurting away. Weaving in and out among the occasional floaters who made up the rest of the mid-week crowd. She moved in extraordinary flights, every way, everywhere.

He tried to keep up with her. His ribs were starting to ache, and he didn't know how *she* was able to stand the pace. But whenever he thought of settling to the bottom, of going to the floor and shucking the weights, of calling time and paying his fee, of going back to the hotel . . . Every time he thought of something like that, he would catch another eyeful of flaming red hair, and he would be after her again.

In time, in weary time, he caught on to the gimmicks of the sport.

Plan ahead. Be quick. Move decisively. Notice that her path is going to be blocked by a heavy old man who is dozing in the air; then head at once, not for her, but for the point of intersection . . .

As he closed in, he took hold of the ropes that attached the weights to her body.

"You can't do that," she announced, trying to break free, whipping the flat side of a hand at his face.

He ducked, talking fast. "My name is Chet McCoy.

Vacationing from Earth orbit. Would you like to know what I did last night?"

The teeth she showed brightly were not part of a smile.

"Damn you, let go!" Pulling, pushing—he liked the feel of that—and letting her anger show in a number of certain terms. "If the manager spots you interfering with my thrust, you'll never get in here again."

"Then you don't want to talk?" Chet said.

"Hell, no."

"Drink?"

"No. Nothing. Leave me alone. You're in trouble, and I can't afford to hang around with you." She got loose, suddenly, with no special effort. She had distracted him with her green eyes and with statements that he couldn't understand. *What did she know about him?*

She shot up and away, edges softened by the mist. Higher. Lower. Finally looking back at him. He spotted her glance; he'd been treading gravless in the same place, sort of giving up on it all. She must have sensed it. With a flip that defied imitation, she halved the distance between them, slowed up, shrugged her shoulders, and pointed down to the floor.

He matched her pace sinking down. The weights provided just enough negative buoyancy that, when left to their own physics, they caused the wearer to settle to the bottom like the sediment in a good Jupiter wine.

He sat on the rubbery floor.

"Hello again," he said. She was too far to touch; close enough, barely, to hear—about four meters away, he guessed, and that was quite a stretch even in negligible gravity.

She said, "Chet, that was your name?"

He nodded.

"Avon Clahr," she told him in return, a little more cordially than when she was up in the air, but still cagey, still very much on guard. He liked her name.

And her red hair, spun down to her neck. And all that.

Avon.

"What I did last night," he explained, "was to check in at the Towers and sleep off the space lag. We could go back there. The bar's got a starry act on the holograph and the lightball courts are open all night."

The first smile arrived on the cream of her skin.

"What was the rest of your name?"

"McCoy. It's an Earth name."

"So what? Chet McCoy—I don't mind Earth names. My father's name, after all, was John. I'm only the first generation here myself, and it takes a hell of a lot more reproductions to get a real native." She kept avoiding his eyes, looking over his shoulder, glancing around nervously. "And don't tell me big things about your hotel. I work there."

He was sure he hadn't seen her. Maybe if she was out of the du-suit and into . . . He couldn't stand the thought. That is, sitting, he couldn't stand it. He stood up. "Doing what?"

She looked up at him. "You name it. I'm an assistant instructor in crater skiing, lightball, and swimming. I have a small part in the live-merge with the holoshow. Other than that I help out in the offices."

"You're just what I need," he said. "Let's go back and you can show me around."

She stood up, too, and began removing the weights.

"No," she said. "I'm not going anywhere with you. It's not that you don't seem like a good guy. But your bodyguards—they're *awful,* and they give me the creeps."

For a moment he didn't know who she was talking about, but then he remembered. He was so used to them, in Earth orbit, on Earth itself, everywhere . . . He was so used to them that he sometimes found them very easy to ignore. They were different faces all the time, but they all played on the same team.

He held up a hand to make her wait, then turned his neck both ways until he picked out the men that she had seen. Still on his tail, all day. Now in their rented du-suits, equipped and attached to the cheaper blue weights: a couple of creepy looking (he had to agree with Avon about that) and hard-nosed characters whose wide striped sideburns were of a style more typical to this part of the galaxy.

"So that's what's bothering you," he said, giving half of his attention back to Avon. "They're not my bodyguards. They're starcops."

She took another look. "Like hell. You're kidding."

He shook his head.

"Look, it's no secret even out here. I'm a bookie. I manage to stay outside the law back on Earth because I operate from *Ruffian*—a satellite—but the cops are always at my door. That's why I had to leave for a while. When Inspector Quill found out that I'd brought in a million-dollar handle on the new Moon-to-Earth freefalls, he turned the whole region of star police into the Vice & McCoy Squad. And these guys—," he jerked his thumb at the two men who now were busy getting rid of their outfits, "—well, it looks like Quill notified the SunStop 6 force to carry on. A pair of flatfooted sixers."

"I don't think so," Avon said. "Your two friends who are sticking so close are not from the starcops."

"No one else would—"

"And they're not sixers, either," she went on. He took a couple of steps toward her, but she moved back to keep the slot open. "This place is full of spies from SunStop 8. People are followed and the followers are followed. It's nothing new to get involved, but it always means trouble, and I don't want any. I can't tell you much about the starcops . . . But hell, Chet, I know eighters when I see them."

"*Eighters?*"

"Of course," she said.

He stared at them again. Physically, he thought, they could be eighters. But logically and practically, there was no reason in the whole chain of SunStops for a connection between him and the eighters. Or any other number. The only person he knew in this double-star area was Avon; and even her, not too long and not too well.

"They can't be eighters," he argued. "I'm on SunStop 6. I've never been to SunStop 8—*never.* And I can't recall it causing any winners or losers that I've booked; it doesn't have any events worth betting on, except overthrowing the government, and that takes too long for my turnover. But that's all I know about SunStop 8. That's all I want to know about eighters. As far as I'm concerned, it's a dead planet in someone else's computer."

"Those two aren't dead," she said earnestly. "And they're sure as hell following *you!*"

"For no reason at all," he replied. No matter how much he looked at their blank and frozen faces, he still thought of them as starcops, his first impression. "What do they want with me?"

She raised her long lashes, letting more green spill out of her eyes.

She said, "Beats me. Take your choice, Chet. If they're not Pawk Ludinder's men, then they could belong to any of a dozen different revolutionary clubs, whichever one is popular today."

Chet searched his mind for the latest political scratch sheet and found that he didn't have one. He was neutral, just like Earth. Let SunStop 8 fight its own internal battles and whoever was on top when it finished hemorrhaging could try to hang on after the innards were healed and restless again . . .

"Sorry, Chet," Avon was saying. "I'm staying clear of people from SunStop 8. They're free and easy with firing squads and assassins and cold dark cells. I don't want to get involved with eighters anywhere. Just don't mix me up in it. *Please*."

"Look. No kidding," he protested. "I'm just a bookie on vacation."

"Well, when you can prove it, when you get rid of your pals—then, what the hell, give me a call." She took a step closer, the closest she'd been since they'd tangled in the warm mist above, and tilted her face to let the moist skin glisten everlastingly in his mind while she put him through a final consideration. If she reached a verdict, he couldn't tell what it was. Maybe he would never know. There was no other word from her; she wheeled and walked away, heading for the cubicle in the corner to turn in the equipment and check out.

He made no effort to go after her. A few minutes later, when he was piling his own du-suit and weights on the counter, he saw a final flash of Avon Clahr's red hair. Out and gone. As if he had never chased her through the hot clouds of SunStop 6, and never again would.

The SaunArena's lights were far behind him and the Towers' beacons were a kilometer ahead. In the place between, where he was traveling at a comfortable speed on the moving walkway, it was almost dark. There was only the glow of the path itself. A place, it seemed to him in his thoroughly rotten mood, that was built for showdowns.

Chet stopped; that is, he stepped off the side of the walkway and ducked into a darker area behind one of the spread trees. It would be the first brawl of his vacation, he thought, but he wasn't out to set a record. Avon had posted the rules—get rid of the eighters. All right . . . For Avon Clahr and for other reasons of equal weight.

Followed all day, and into the night, and even into

the air, by two unknown space-chewers . . . It was time to find out why. A fist in their faces could bring on some answers.

And that would be his first offer.

He took deep breaths while he waited, feet spread, hands knotted, ready to take apart his double shadows. He would get one of them from behind, he figured, and after he put that one out of action, he would deal indelicately with the one that was still conscious. . .

Only they weren't there. Now that he wanted them, now that he needed them . . . *Now* they were out for a short beer. For twenty minutes more Chet's gray eyes probed the dim aura of the walkway. The lack of expected targets mixed like Venusian bees with the ready energies of his nerve ends; but there was nothing. Finally, his mood no better but no worse, he returned to the glow of the path and moved along to the hotel. At the base of the Towers' main spindle, he stopped again to look around. There was still no sign of the two men. Nor was there much chance of finding them in the midst of the Towers: the three hundred and seven spindles created a maze that would baffle a hungry rat, and it was only the computer, working with the microcode on the bottom of Chet's shoes, that led him to his own riser. Going up in the tube to his spool on the forty-fourth, he felt himself beginning to relax. *Could he find Avon again? Tonight?* The tube opened directly into the exact center of his revolving suite, and the lights went on automatically as he walked in.

They were waiting for him.

One on the bed and one in a chair, sitting with crossed legs and the familiar blank faces. They were back in their regular clothes which were two shades of brown in the form of loose jackets. Their accessories for the evening were guns.

Chet recognized a conventional blaster in the bigger man's hand, while the other had a pistol that might have shot chemopellets.

The man in the chair, the big man with the blaster, uncrossed his legs and put his weight forward on the soles of his feet. His feet were the right size to take all that weight.

He said, "Pack your clothes, McCoy."

"Are you part of the tour?" Chet wanted to know. "I think I'd rather have a free squeezebag of gin. Can I take it up with the director?"

"Don't argue. Pack them up. You're checking out."

"But, pal, I just got here." Stalling, Chet was not surprised to find that the feisty spirit he'd left outside on the walkway was seeking him out in a manner well enlivened by frustration. It was difficult for him to keep his hands open; he waved at the walls of the room, a moving circle of glass through which shone bright images of other SunStops bordered by the flickering of unfamiliar stars. "Where else can you get this view?" he rambled on. "And down below they have a pool with hot running women."

They refused to look at anything but Chet. The man on the bed, smaller but with death in his voice, checked the time and issued his own version of the invitation. "Hurry up. Your bags are there."

"Where am I going?"

"You might find out."

"When?"

"When you get there. *If* you get there."

"I'll get there all right. It's your ugly heads that will . . ." Chet faded out the threat with a look that filled it back in. His arms were aching, and it wasn't from the SaunArena. What was the score? he wondered, as he put his largest suitcase on the bench. Why the clothes? Why pack for a one-way trip? And if they weren't taking him for a kill, then what were they taking him for, or to, or into, or away from? Ransom? Who would pay a dollar for a bookie? Mistaken identity? No, they called him by name, and he was well enough known wherever he went. Then, dammit, why?

Mentally, Chet shook his head. In each eye was an eighter and a gun, and in the beat of his heart was the hope of handling them. Now his teeth were starting to hurt; it was either talk or fight. Or both.

"It's going to be tough to leave," he began, at the same time he dropped in the last shirt. "You know how it is, you wait *years* to come to a place like Sun-Stop 6." He closed the bag. "And finally you're here at—what do they call it?—*the scene of a thousand and one emotions*, ready to take on anything." He snapped the lock and curled his fingers around the handle. "Including stardust idiots like you," he said . . . And he threw the full suitcase half the length of the room and right into the meaty chest of the man in the chair.

With almost the same movement, Chet was diving onto the bed.

He tackled the stunned man who sat there. His knee pinned the gun hand while he let a forearm fly into the throat, cutting off a breath in progress and a few yet to come. He followed it with a tightly balled right hand that landed square and knuckled on the man's nose, bringing forth a spurt of red blood to go with his coughing jag.

More, Chet urged himself.

Putting his whole weight into the mattress, he gathered himself like a spring and let loose in a leap that carried him in full flight to the man in the chair. The big man had just disentangled himself from the loaded suitcase and was raising the blaster when Chet plowed into him with a hard-driving shoulder. The chair tipped backwards. Then it broke apart and they both went sprawling. Wrestling for his life on the floor, Chet was too tight in a clinch to land any blows, so he concerned himself with getting to the gun first.

Suddenly he saw that it was too late.

The small man, with his battered and bleeding face, was off the bed, rearmed and charging to help his partner. Chet already had both hands full with an eighter and a gun. In the rotating background of star-dappled space, he saw the other eighter coming, he saw the other gun coming; and, he reflected darkly, there wasn't a goddamn thing he could do about it.

2.
The Brauna Test

Brauna, the blonde, was sleeping. Sleeping hard or faking it. This in itself was no problem because Rocky had been reviving girls since June of 2057.3.

"Hey, baby," he said, reaching for her bare stomach. "If you don't wanna—"

He stopped short. His arm froze as if someone had grabbed his wrist. He cocked his head, wrinkling his wide nose, listening to a taped voice that was triggered automatically every time all the weight went to one side of the bed.

"Even amazonic blondes need a coffee break once in a while. It's not their fault that you were born and bred a Wiggeneer. You're a big load for a woman to carry all night and all day. Leave her alone." Chet McCoy had said all that, sounding even bossier on tape than he did in person. *"And remember, you've got other things to do."*

"Aw, stick a pod up your tubes," Rocky replied aloud. Chet was light-years away on SunStop 6, and his crummy lectures could go just as far and never come back.

Continuing to grumble, he took a last futile look at the rise and fall of the breasts in his bed. He liked girls whose chests heaved amply. The motion reminded him of his native planet. The memory of Wiggen's sighing wellsprings started to calm him down. He swung his hairy legs off the bed and stuck them into a pair of white shorts.

Anyway, he thought resignedly, it was high time he checked on what gave with the law.

He left his compartment, bedroom number two, and walked into *Ruffian's* control room, more commonly known as the tote board. Nobody was there of course. The starcops would have a tough time getting a warrant to barge into a private satellite, although they sometimes managed to pay an informal visit. Most often they just circled outside in juxtaposition or planted electronic gadgets on *Ruffian's* antennas. This week . . . Would they be back? Rocky wondered. He fell into the chair at the console and turned on the 'scopes.

He grinned.

Clear. *Six, two, and even,* according to the computer that figured the odds. There were no objects in range, in any concentric orbit. Nearby space was empty.

He waited. It stayed empty.

He shut off the equipment and returned to the bedroom.

After a shake and a pinch and a bellow in her ear, Brauna stirred from her coma and sat up, rubbing everything she had a pair of, from her eyes on down. And her sigh of relief came from the fact that Rocky was standing and that he was clad where it counted.

"Go away," she said. "I'm sore all over."

"Too much sleep," Rocky offered innocently.

She sat straighter. "Sleep? I haven't had any sleep since the night I broke the quad on your head."

"Yeah. You notice there ain't no more music in here now'days . . . C'mon, get up. We gotta do the phone bit."

"Not that again? It's the most ridiculous—"

"Gotta be done," he said firmly. "But it'll be the last time if we still don't get no answer."

"And if we get an answer, we'll get a fire ship. And foam! We'll get covered with sticky foam and they'll inject it inside and my clothes will get ruined and my hair will turn brown and my skin will break out–"

"C'mon, doll. We gotta do it, like Chet says."

She buried her face in her hands for a full minute. When she looked up again, the fear of foam was gone from her eyes.

"Oh, all right, Rocky," she said. "But then I'm taking an ultrabath." With both hands on the mattress, she pushed herself off the bed and, standing slowly, seemed to rise higher and higher and higher.

She was a big woman. The Rock himself had muscles rippling from both ends of his white shorts, a body cut from a quarry, but he didn't have much height; so his square-cut face and Brauna's gentler oval face were on separate levels, and the closely cropped hair on his head was just high enough to tickle her nose. Which was all right in its way because more often than not Brauna liked having her nose aroused.

Wiggling all the way, she followed him back to the control room. She had not put any clothes on. None were wanted for the phone bit and none were needed for the following ultrabath or for whatever Rocky had in mind. Arriving at the console, she pushed away the seat that was in front of the telecommunicator, and she put her feet precisely onto the floor markings. She touched a hand to her blonde hair.

"I could get in trouble," she said, hesitating.

Rocky's jaw dropped. "I thought you was taking those pills!"

"I mean about this transmission. If the fire ship really comes. . ."

"Don't worry about the fire ship. I'll take care of the fire ship. You just do the yelling, and give it all you got."

"Well, if you're sure," she said. She arranged her hair again. Then she put her hands on her bare hips, screwed her face into a terrified grimace, and opened her eyes as wide as they would go. "OK, I'm ready."

"Hold on a sec," Rocky warned her. He touched the console lights, activating *Ruffian's* four private communication channels: to Earth, to other vehicles in orbit, to the moon and its relay station for the solar system, and the AmDrive interstellar beam. All but the last would get a picture of the naked Brauna, but the outer galaxy would have to settle for her voice alone . . . *if* anyone was eavesdropping. When the channels were all verified for security and privacy, Rocky sliced a finger at Brauna's face. "Go ahead, doll."

Raising her arms high above her head, with her breasts riding along, she screwed on her wild expression and yelled to the universe: "Help! I've been raped and we're on fire! Help me, please—hurry! Fire! We're trapped! We can't last much longer! Help! There's fire all over . . . and I'm sore all over!"

Rocky disconnected the transmission and waved his arm sideways to cut her off. She leaned forward onto his shoulder, letting out a deep breath, exhausted. He gave her a kiss on the cheek.

"Good, real good," he said. "That was the best you ever done. But you didn't have to add that bit about being sore."

"Well, I am," she replied, and left him there.

He watched her shimmy off to the bathroom, and then he swiveled the chair back toward the console. He switched the communicator to receiving mode. He turned on all of the 'scopes. He put his feet up and waited.

An hour later, he heard no alarms and there were no ships in sight. Rocky gave it another twenty minutes before he was sure and satisfied. But that seemed to be it: now a week had gone by with no watchdogs in orbit and no taps on the communicator and, best of all, no Inspector Quill. The full test sequence that Chet had created before he left had been run through, with results that called for a drink or at least a boozer pill; and it happened that Rocky was ready with one of each. He washed down the pill, took a last look at the console lights, shut off everything, and smiled.

The tests were over.

The heat was off.

The law had gone away.

Quill and his starcops had given up.

The next step? Rocky snapped his fingers as the thought popped up in his brain, a vision of special events that would put things back to normal. First, get a message to Chet on SunStop 6 that the sky was cool. It had to be, Chet would return on the next flight. It had to be, Earth's busiest bookies would be back in business . . . The deedee races at Belmont Studios, the San Andreas quake numbers, the freefalls, the Comet Corps and the rival Grandmother League, the UN sweepstakes . . . It had to be soon. Because when it's out of money, the Rock told himself, then it's bye-bye Brauna.

He glanced in the direction of the bathroom. The trouble with ultrabaths is that they could last forever and felt as good as sex. But—he snapped his fingers—first things first.

Get the word to Chet.

Even though interstellar transmission rode along on the AmDrive beam, using the same skip principles as the fleet itself, there was no way to get around the nine-minute lag that was left after remote condensation. It took patience to talk to the outer galaxy; usually you brought along something to read during the conversation.

Wiggeneers could read if they wanted to. Usually they didn't want to. Rocky just spent the phone time eyeing the corridor and playing an imaginary drum on the console.

"There's no answer on your call to SunStop 6," the operator said sweetly.

Rocky grunted. "Whadayamean, no answer? It's a hotel. It gotta be there."

Eighteen minutes later the blue light flickered.

"No answer in the *room*, sir. I reached the Towers, but Mr. McCoy doesn't answer the phone in his room."

"Well, have him paged," suggested the Rock. "Do I gotta tell you how to do your thing?"

Eighteen minutes more.

"We're paging him now. I'll call you back, sir."

"You bet," said Rocky, and he pressed the PAUSE stud. He swung around in the chair to leer toward the bathroom, and shortly afterward he was shouting through the locked door. "Hey, doll, you been in there long enough to get turned inside out."

"And I'm staying in here," Brauna replied. "I'm sore all over and I know what you want. Did a fire ship come?"

"Naw, and there's no foam. C'mon out. You gotta come out sometime."

"Not until you promise to leave me alone for the rest of the day."

"I ain't making no promises."

"Then I'm not coming out, Rocky. I'm—"

"I know, I know. Sore all over." He shook his head disappointedly. "You got the build, yeah . . . But not the guts."

In the middle of that Wiggeneer philosophy he heard the buzzer sounding in the control room. He gave the bathroom door a last rattle, squinting at the number plate and trying to remember the code that opened it. But it had rarely ever been locked. He shrugged, scratching his forehead. *Maybe he could ask Chet!* He scrambled back to the buzzing console.

It was a different operator with the same kind of message.

"On your call to SunStop 6, sir. I'm sorry, but Mr.

McCoy has not responded to the page in any part of the Towers."

"Well, so he's out someplace," Rocky informed her without much concern. "Do me a favor, doll. Will you keep trying every hour till you get him? I'll be right here all the time."

Eighteen minutes later she promised to take care of it.

He switched off, content with his efforts, a little worried about the expense of the interstellar phone bill, and recalled the last of Chet's instructions. No bookmaking until Chet came back to take over. That left a few more days with nothing special to do. *Wait a minute,* Rocky reversed himself. A guy who thinks a giant blonde is nothing special is a guy who ain't been taking his vitamins.

He hitched up his shorts and moved over to the computer terminal. Eagerly, he began to punch the keys. He wondered why girls get sore and why girls get stubborn, and he wondered why girls don't take sonic showers like everybody else—but he knew this much: somewhere out on the computer's microchip was the code key to the bathroom door.

3.
830754 and Then Some

Both suns were blazing through the open window. Chet McCoy had never seen a pattern of shadows like the crisscross that covered the room.

In addition to multiple shadows the room had four walls, one mirrored, and a few scattered pieces of expensive-looking furniture. There was no sign of artificial lighting, which meant that solar energy was being absorbed by the outside walls for use during the short night; the ideal situation for the SunStops. In the far corner on a pedestal Chet saw a holosquare containing the lifelike head of an archetypal hero. In the opposite corner was a tall table with a tall vase and seemingly short flowers. And the bed he was in had a roof on it, quilted at that.

It was a nice place to visit, but he didn't want to die there.

He got off the bed. He didn't move beyond that until his head cleared; then he went looking for his clothes. All he found was an android, size extra-large, who was kneeling in front of the closet.

And who talked, metallically. "An Octo welcome to you, McCoy. I am putting your shoes away. I am 830754."

Chet could see the name for himself. The six digits had been electronically embroidered on the side of the android's thick neck. As 830754 got up from his knees, Chet found the rest of him to be a massively architectured structure with a stoic face and no hair.

"I am here to take care of you," the android continued. "Are you ready for a bath and a shave, or would you prefer breakfast first? We have toilets nearby."

"Well, flush me some bacon and eggs," Chet responded levelly.

"I can do that, but they will be synthetics. The pigs and chickens are all gone."

"Gone? Where'd they go?" A strange place, Chet thought, as the last of the wake-up pain eased out of the back of his head.

830754 bent his wide shoulders. "I do not know. No one knows. We revolt to get real food, we win, we get great quantities of real food to celebrate the victory, and then—poof—the pigs and chickens are gone again."

"So are my things," Chet pointed out.

"No, no. Your things are here—*there*."

The android was referring to a foldout dresser which was the only item of furniture set against the mirrored wall. In the top drawer Chet found his money and comb and keys; the next drawer contained the disposable shirts and shorts and such. He assumed that everything else was stowed in the closet.

Closing the dresser drawers, Chet scanned the room again from wall to wall, and stopped when he got to the android. "Can you tell me exactly where I am?" he asked.

"We have toilets nearby," replied 830754, dwelling on the merits of the place as if to make up for the lack of pigs and chickens.

"Nearby to what?"

"What?"

"I asked you first," Chet said. He pointed to the window. "Look, I can see that I'm on one of the SunStops, and I can guess that it's SunStop 8 because I was snatched by a pair of eighters. But all that doesn't cancel my rights to the question . . . Where am I?"

The android seemed surprised. "This is Decatur."

"Is it?" Chet said; but of course it had to be. He considered it further. Before all the infighting and terror and death had turned SunStop 8 into a boycotted planet, it had been the prime resort of the galaxy. The most fun. The best weather. The tops in food, gambling, and wild entertainment. In line with that goal, and unaware of the coming conflicts that would ravage the city, the original colonists had picked the obvious name for the capitol of the swingingest, boom-boom wonderplanet—*Decatur*. The phrase that went with it, archaic and almost forgotten, had immediately rippled through the colonized worlds with all the charm of its original meaning . . . *an eighter from Decatur*. Born of dice, or craps, whatever; Chet knew it well.

"The capitol city of SunStop 8," he said aloud. "And this, I'll bet, is the capitol building."

And in the time it took to say it, his mind raced around and around, and it came out here: *Decatur itself*. Through all the revolutions, always the capitol, always the headquarters of whichever group seized the power. Symbolic of victory. Also, in Chet's case, complete with a super servant and a luxurious room that he hadn't earned on his good looks alone. But why the royal carpet for a hostage, or whatever he was? He had the feeling that it might be a short jump from royal house to rough house, and that feeling came partly from the impression that 830754 was much more of a guardian than a servant.

Chet looked toward the window. The frame of sky was clear and very blue.

"Maybe I'm the first in a drastic plan to bring back the tourists," he mused aloud. "Okay, 830—," he turned to get a look at the android's neck, "—754, while I'm out charging a sackful of souvenirs, you get me a seat on the next AmDrive flight to Earth."

"There are no such flights from here," was the reply.

"Then I'll take a pod back to SunStop 6."

"Ah, no such pods. None that are commercial."

"Well, a military flight, then, or one from the government. I don't care. Where's the embassy?"

The android hesitated until something clicked. "The Earth embassy? There has not been one for quite some time. Very few embassies in Decatur. Earth and the other SunStops do not engage in anything with us because of their conflict with Pawk Ludinder."

"Look, I've got to get back one way or another," Chet said. "What do you suggest?"

"A bath and breakfast. Ludinder will see you afterward."

"I get to see *Ludinder*?"

"That is correct," said 830754.

Chet gave it some thought. All bets were off until he changed the odds. A meeting with the top man seemed as improbable as the rest of the caper, but if Chet had any complaints (and he had a *couple*), Pawk Ludinder was the man to take them to. Complaints get action at the summit. On the other hand, he reasoned coldly, there was a vicious rumor brewing Earthside that most complaints on SunStop 8 were handled in a manner leading directly to a blindfold and a last request . . . For the next twenty minutes the thought of a firing squad rested uncomfortably in the foreground of his brain.

As he acquainted himself with the plumbing.

As he got dressed: Slip-on shoes, dark pants, and a shirt sealed midway up the front.

As he consumed something that looked like an omelette but tasted like fried leaves off a spread tree.

As he was allowed a second cup of coffee.

After which 830754 announced: "McCoy, you are ready to meet Ludinder."

Chet sprawled in the chair that had been set up next to his bed, and looked at the android with an expression that he expected was both firm and cynical.

"That's what you think," he said. "I'm not ready to meet him or anyone. I'm only ready to get out of here. I don't like the way I got to SunStop 8, and I don't like eighters for the same reasons. I don't like important people like Pawk Ludinder, and I don't like this pompous bedroom you've signed me up for, and especially, 830754, I don't like the way you handle a sonic shave."

"Tomorrow you may shave yourself," the android compromised. It was impossible to ever see any emotion on his face, and Chet couldn't guess whether the same flatness extended to the clockworks inside. The eyes—what color were the eyes? Black? Dark brown? "Unless, McCoy, you are too busy by then and request that I continue my services."

Chet perked up. "Busy? Busy doing what?"

"Ludinder will tell you."

"*You* tell me. C'mon, you're a servant, you're an android, you give shaves and all that . . . C'mon, you tell me."

"I cannot say."

Chet's gray eyes narrowed into slits of anger.

He stood up. "I say you can say. You know damn well what this is all about. It's odds-on that you helped write the script. Android or not, you sure can do a lot better than mourning the pigs and touting the toilets!"

The large servant looked down at him.

"Ludinder will tell you," he repeated. Somehow the voice that was always the same tone managed to convey a stern message when it was necessary.

Chet walked around the chair and went to the window, gazing out into a number-one day in the shine of the suns, but comprehending far less of the landscape than of his own pounding thoughts. Enough was enough. *How did he get into this?* But no more, no deeper. He knew from a lifetime of battles that he was in a situation where he couldn't set his own rules; still, he didn't intend to go on being a patsy, tossed around at their whims and for their unknown purposes.

Already he'd been cut from his loving, abbreviated from his vacation, bashed by a gun butt, and shanghaied to a tension planet. The wounds were deep. Before he collected any more of them, he was going to initiate a few of his own. At the rate of two for one.

Easing back into the center of the room, he staged a dramatic confrontation with the android. A stiff finger went straight into the servant's chest. "As far as I'm concerned," Chet said, "your big boss Pawk Ludinder is a damned space-chewer, and I'm not going anywhere in his direction. Do you understand that?"

"You will go, if I have to drag you." Something clicked in the android's dark eyes. "Or even if I have to carry you."

"No, you don't," Chet told him, standing obstinately in front of him. "You can't touch me. You're not human—you're an android. An automaton. A big, electromechanical number-name. I'll give you the orders, pal, and you follow them."

830754 blinked.

Then he tried to frown. Maybe he was confused by all of Chet's rules, or maybe he was just running out of patience. But whatever the reason, he took a giant step forward that brought them toe-to-toe; he stood there for a moment, moving his wide chin back and forth like a pendulum ticking to a bomb, and then he threw an open hand in a wicked arc that exploded on Chet's face . . . and almost tore it off.

Picking himself up from the floor, Chet tried to shake off the sting. But he couldn't stop the pain any more than he could stop his blood from roaring. All right, he thought. Things were lining up in their corners. And soon. Pretty goddamn soon. . .

When he looked up again, it was with the trace of a piratic smile. "Friends no more, huh?"

"I just do my job," the android said, back to no visible expression. "Are you ready to go now?"

"I suppose it's either that or turn the other cheek."

The striking hand poised again. "Which will it be?"

"Well, it isn't that I give a damn about your threats, but I only have one cheek left and I need it for being conceited." Chet raised his own hand; half a wave and half a mock salute. "Give me the directions, and I'll go say 'Octo' to good old Ludinder."

Instantly the android latched onto Chet's shoulders with a grip like a gantry crane. "I will take you there," he said, and his two strong, pushing hands showed that he meant it. But Chet put on the brakes before they reached the door.

"Wait a minute," was his protest. "These aren't my walking shoes. These are only for the bedroom. I need a pair with air chambers."

The servant looked down at Chet's feet. "Why, McCoy?"

"Because I've got fallen arches," Chet said.

830754 produced a mechanical sigh. The empty face he wore was not a true measure of his feelings. He released his hold on Chet's arms and stood by, grumbling in his internal language.

Planning ahead, Chet walked to the closet.

He slid open one door just far enough to display the shoe rack. He knelt in front of it. Barely moving his arm, he picked out one black shoe and with a twist of his wrist threw it into the dark end of the closet. Then he leaned in farther, rummaging wildly. Finally he pounded his fist on the floor, turned around, still kneeling, and said in scolding words: "What did you do with my other shoe?"

"Your shoe?" asked 830754.

"My *other* shoe," Chet explained. He kept his voice hard and demanding. "My other shoe, pal. It looks like this one, but it's the other one."

"It is there. I remember putting them both there."

"When was that?"

"This morning, McCoy. You saw me putting them all there."

Chet considered it. "And who's been in here since?"

"No one but you and I."

"So, goddammit. . . ."

"So," said the android, "it must be there."

Chet spread his hands. "Easy for you to say. But it's *not* there. And if you knew anything about my feet, you'd know that I can't walk very far or stand for very long without my good air shoes. If you really want me to get to see Ludinder, you better come up with my other shoe."

"Bah!" The android was close to an explosion of parts. He strode to the closet. He was sure that he hadn't miscounted; it was not possible for him to miscount. He was sure that this Earthman named Chet McCoy was partly insane and totally a troublemaker. And he was sure, above all, in and out of all his circuits, that the missing footwear was someplace in the closet.

Grunting, he gestured Chet aside and dug in.

Chet stepped aside. Far enough aside to reach the tall vase that was pointing up from the corner table. From there he could see 830754 down on his knees, scrounging under the shoe rack.

Chet lifted the vase. With a hand at each end, he turned it horizontally and carried it, one quiet step at a time, to his target. Once there, he took quick aim and let it go. He didn't just drop it on the android's square head—he *mashed* it into the back of the skull. He hadn't seen so many pieces since the night he pulled Rocky out of the Martian whoredome.

Rocky? Back on Ruffian *with all the boozer pills and no idea that . . .*

After a violent spasm of the whole body, 830754's legs shot straight out, and he went to sleep with his nose in the closet, the numbers on his neck stretched out to higher values. If androids have dreams . . . Well, thought Chet, it served him right.

He plucked a set of plastic cards from the servant's pocket and took them to the bedroom's outer door. The fourth card he tried caused the slot to respond with a whirring connection which freed the knob.

Opening the door to the width of his face, Chet peered through the gap. *Sonuvabitch!* He closed the door immediately and leaned against it, breathing a little harder. He spread the key cards in his fingers and studied them like a bust poker hand. He couldn't believe the rotten luck. He'd come a barrel of light-years to get away from cops at his door . . . And here he was, with a cop at the door.

4.
A Real Book Lover

He had to get out of the room.

The window was wide open and overlooked the lawn, but there was a long and sheer drop, and the nearest spread tree was impossibly out of reach. That was the score, current and total. It didn't take much handicapping to decide that the door was the one and only reasonable exit. And waiting on the other side was a watchdog with a blaster.

Still, he had to get out of the room.

Once again, slowly and carefully, he opened the door to the same narrow view. The man in uniform, a soldier of the state, sneaked a look back at him from the corner of an eye, then made a stiff left turn, snapping a hand to the gun clip. The sudden reach for the blaster didn't make it easy for Chet to finish the smile he started.

"Easy, pal," he said with what was left. "We've got a little problem in here, and I'm just looking for some help. Can you take time out for an errand of mercy?"

The soldier's chin cut a tough angle. "I'm not allowed to talk to you."

"The errand of mercy I have in mind," Chet explained, "does not involve talking to me."

"Good." The man pulled in his stomach and said nothing further. His eyes and stance went back to his duty. His hand remained on the gun. All that was offered to Chet was a shoulder patch designed in red around the loops of a number eight.

Chet edged open the door another degree.

"Do you know 830754?"

"Yes, the android," replied the soldier with clipped words and a closed mouth.

"He's in here."

"Supposed to be."

Chet nodded. "He was also supposed to find my shoe, but he didn't. Instead, he got a headache and he sort of stretched out on the floor, and I'm afraid he's going to stay down there until he dies or until somebody picks him up . . . And if you've never tried to pick up an android by yourself, then you probably don't know, but you can get ruined for life. It's all that electromechanical stuff inside."

"Inside?" The man turned his head just a bit, still trying not to acknowledge the conversation. "Inside what?"

"Inside the goddamn room, on the floor by the closet," Chet said. He pulled open the door the rest of the way and extended his other arm like an arrow toward the point of impact. "*Over there!*"

Alertly, eyes following the arrow, the soldier spotted the fallen android lying in the midst of the scattered vase. For an instant he seemed to ponder it like a page from basic training; then, skilled in emergencies and paid for quick action, he spread his arms with the passion of a Saturnian mother, dug his boots into the carpeting, and launched himself to the aid of the stricken automaton.

All of which left Chet feeling somewhat ignored. He walked out of the bedroom, quietly closing the door on the first-aid scene behind him. . .

The corridors of the capitol were wide and well lighted. Chet reasoned right from the start of his exploration that there was no chance of him lurking in dark corners, so he chose a path right down the middle. An eighter from Decatur, on a bold and unguided tour of the building . . . He passed a repairman who was up on GravLad fixing the sunbeam, and later he was himself passed by two office workers, plain-looking females, who were carrying their voice notebooks and the kind of pocket calculators that could be tuned to a computer frequency. Every so often he would also come across a dignitary, an official member of the SunStop 8 government; some of them were polite enough to return his nod. A thin crowd, altogether, and a mixture. But what he saw added up to this: *he wasn't going far.* Every archway out of the building was stacked with militia. Even if he had a gate pass, what would it mean? A ticket to nothing. A short walk in a continuous circle. For beyond the gates lay the city of Decatur and the rest of SunStop 8, unmapped to him, a dangerous planet always in the throes of upheaval, with no friendly contacts and no commercial transportation to anywhere he might want to go. The score was getting higher and harder. He knew exactly where he was, but he was lost just the same. He kept walking. Through the hallways, up and down the escalators, and around each and every corner. He kept walking.

A half hour later he was standing in another wing of the building, listening with some disbelief to revved-up sounds that were coming from the other side of an unmarked door. Music it was, loud. At least double quad.

It all registered on a waiting slot in his mind. The triple beat, the low booming voice—*he knew, he knew*—had to come from the old quad viewtapes of Carter Lee Cash! And anyone who played Earth music of that type and that vintage, at that volume, in this place, might be someone who was not under the control of Pawk Ludinder. Someone, maybe, who could help.

But there was no name on the door.

Chet pushed it open and went in. He was glad he did. The music lover was a girl, a woman. Sitting cross-legged on the floor with a book in her lap, reading in the light of the flashing wall screens, swaying, he reflected, to the tempo of hard Cash beats. She had all the right melodies. She had everything.

She looked up through long lashes.

"Octo, sweetie," she yelled over the noise. "Drop down here and give me a hand."

"Yeah," he said uncomfortably. He looked for numbers on her neck. There were none. She was *real*.

A brunette, not the sort men dream about, but her body was the kind you have to see to know you want it, and that you've wanted it—*always*. Kittenish, she might have been called, from the bare toes to the dark brown hair that swirled in a natural wave around a white headband. Chet went on staring. Her breasts were small but well emphasized, as if she iced the nipples every hour on the hour, and they were loose beneath the cross-seal of her blouse, itself tucked into a tiny belt at the waist. All that and more. Without moving a single centimeter she nevertheless seemed to be lunging at him . . .

He sat down on the floor by her side.

"What do you need?"

"Need?" she replied with an appropriate look in her eyes.

"You said to give you a hand."

"Sure, sweetie. Put it in mine." Swinging her shoulders to the rhythmic pulse of the lights and music, she swiveled to partly face him, and he gave her his hand. She wrapped it in both of hers, holding it on top of the book. "I know who you are. You're the Earthman gambler and your name is McCrory."

"Mc*Coy*," he corrected her. "And I'm a bookie."

"Isn't that what I said? Phooey. It doesn't matter. I'm Juell, you know, and you can listen or read."

"What are you reading?"

"Nothing you'd like, sweetie. It's a programming manual. For the computer. I'm trying to figure out how to open the vault. I may not be able to do it, it's very hard to understand." She squeezed his hand tighter leaning forward to study his face. "How long does Ludinder want you to stay?"

"I wouldn't know," he replied, matching her study for study and squeeze for squeeze. If it wasn't for her mention of Ludinder, he might have been able to forget that he was some kind of escaped prisoner who was probably being hunted down from room to room, and any minute this might be the room.

"He should have told you how long, I would think," she said.

"Maybe so, Juell, but I haven't seen him yet."

"You haven't seen Ludinder?"

"No."

"But . . . then where is the android?"

"If you mean 830754, the last time I saw him he was lying in my closet. I was the center of all his attention, but he was just a number to me."

Juell laughed. "You killed him?"

"No, I don't think so," Chet said, hoping for the best. He didn't need a dead android at this spin of the wheel. "But I destroyed a vase. It could have been an antique."

"Good for you, Chet." She stopped laughing, and the music boomed by itself for a few seconds, until she joined it again with a more serious set of lyrics. "I *despise* antiques. If I could, I would destroy them all myself. Being old is being useless . . . being ugly and mean . . . being lost. There are so many old things in my life right now . . . But then, I forgot; you haven't met him yet."

"Met who?"

"My husband," she said acidly. "Pawk Ludinder."

Chet pulled his hand out of her lap and stared at her, stunned.

She seemed to fade away like a bad dream in the morning; but the shock was only a temporary relief, and as he stared and stared she emerged from his mind's blur as a real nightmare. *Of all the goddamn places to be!* As if he wasn't in enough trouble, as if it hadn't already been all winter in a day, now . . . *now* he was making time with the dictator's wife. *Hallelunar!*

Even the quad system was pushed to its limit.

Chet heard the music fade to the last gasping upbeat; then the walls became white and the whole thing clicked off. But if silence was a blessing, Juell was an atheist. Undaunted, she reached behind her for the remote control, covered a light with her thumb, and covered it again for a track change. Once more music echoed from wall to wall. And those walls turned colors and seemed to go in and out like they were panting for breath; an illusion, Chet thought, that worked to much better effect than his own set back on *Ruffian*. You had to feel it. No matter what.

Juell was turned on, too.

"Go ahead, Chet, run away," she shouted. "Run like all the others do. Bury your head and close your eyes and grow deaf, and pretend that I don't exist." She breathed her breasts to a defiant angle that yanked the blouse from her waist. "There isn't a man on SunStop 8 who is brave enough to touch me!" She collapsed inward again. "Or even talk to me," she added sadly.

Chet was standing up, a good three steps away from her.

"Well, honey," he said. "I might believe in living dangerously, but I don't believe in suicide. When it comes to guys and other men's wives, it's for sure the survival of the fleetest. And that goes double when she's married to a man who owns an army."

"Married, phooey! He's a shriveled old man."

"Did you just find that out?"

Juell stood up with him, leaving the computer manual on the floor. Wicked colors snapped around her face. The music floated with her voice. "It was a marriage of convenience, sweetie. No—why should I say that?—it was a necessity. It serves its purpose. After all, I am the First Lady of SunStop 8."

Stepping forward, she neared him until they were as close as they'd been while they were on the floor. Her lips came very close to his. Any closer, he thought, and he'd be able to talk with her tongue. True enough, her sticks and stones were melting his bones, and, in marrow and gristle, he needed to retaliate by removing her headband and taking her back down to the floor where right in the midst and memories of old viewtapes from Earth . . . But even in that fever he was nagged to the core by this: he was a fugitive trapped in a maze of unknown trouble, a quandary that any moment could snap out his life; therefore, by all odds, it was *not* time to go to bed.

He managed to keep his hands at his side. Mind over organic matter. Some First Lady! She was his cross, and how he itched to find out whether he could bear her.

"Maybe, Chet," she was saying, "you can help me with this book. I need to open the vault."

He said, "Not now, honey. First things first. How do I get out of here?"

Juell's hands went to her hips. "There's the door."

"That's not what I meant," he told her. "I want to get out of the building, out of Decatur, off of SunStop 8 . . . I don't care where, to any other goddamn planet."

"And you haven't seen Ludinder?"

"No."

"Then you'll never get out of this building alive."

"It's that tough?"

"McCrory," she said, "it's just that tough."

He had to take her word for it. It went along with his own observations; he remembered the passageways and the guards. Tight security. And if he couldn't get out alive, there wasn't much point in getting out. Dead men, he was sure, make lousy bookies and have an empty sex life; and while there may have been a promise of greener grass on the other side of the fence, he damn well wanted to avoid being buried under it.

Spinning mentally in place, Chet marshaled the simple facts. The conclusion was inevitable. But when all the other cards in the deck are worse, when the deft fingers of fate are shuffling, and you're down to your last superdollar . . . Why not just play the hand you're dealt?

"Sure, why not?" he said aloud.

Juell raised a brow, but he didn't let her ask.

"All right, I'm off to see the wizard," he continued. "But it's not my first choice. Tell me, Juell, where does he keep his shriveled body?"

She seemed more pleased than scorned.

"Go past the double doors at the end of the hall," she explained, and her small hand touched his arm. "Don't underestimate Pawk Ludinder. Remember that he led a great revolution, inspiring thousands of eighters to fight and kill and die. And now he tells them exactly how to live, and they listen. He looks like a junkyard, but he has the touch of a devil. Please do as he says, Chet."

Chet gave her a reckless smile. "Sure, honey. As long as he says, 'Earthman, go home.'"

"Do you think he brought you here just for a chat?" she scolded. "Phooey! Listen to me, sweetie. You'll be okay if you follow his orders. Do it, bow to him. Let him be *your* leader."

"That's probably good advice," Chet answered pensively. "But it'll get my blood up."

She sighed. "Fine. I'll be right here waiting for you." She had a way of generating heat that was beyond the plain overlay of her clothes, and beyond the latest in solar strategies. *Beat it,* Chet told himself. *Scram.*

He kissed her lightly on the lips—any more would have crashed the thermostat—and went out the door in a hurry. He began walking to meet his master of the moment, forcing his mind to attend to his doubtful destiny; but still thinking of Juell, still blinking at the pulsating wall lights, still hearing the electronic speed-beats of Carter Lee Cash . . . Maybe it wasn't the relics of Earth Music. Maybe it was the eighter love call.

5.
The Eighter Dictator

Beyond the double doors was a vestibule-in-the-round where Chet was stopped by a pair of husky patriots on patrol. They both pointed their blasters at the home of Chet's last supper, and then went on to search him for concealed weapons. When they found his ID card, they got very excited. "You're McCoy!" one of them said.

Chet took his card back. "Can't deny it. Is there a guy around here named Pawk Ludinder?"

"Ludinder is our president," the other guard replied, and then he said, "Ludinder is a great man."

"I'll decide that for myself, pal," Chet replied, and then realized that he was in for a quick decision. A guard moved up to meet him on each side. Squeezing, pushing, they practically carried him through the other door into the adjacent room; and once inside the royal chamber, they set him down and stepped away, and he was left out in the open, easy to see and be seen.

Big, was his first impression. *Tacky*, was his second.

All around him, white plastic beams curved up to the high domed ceiling. From the dome hung the eighter flag in full red glory (worth a second look). Between the supporting beams, strung out at eye level, were a series of electronicaides as well as three window-size display screens that showed pictures of him from three different angles. Beyond the last screen and off to his right, he noticed that a missing beam disturbed the symmetry of walls, and in its place was a pair of du-metal doors, solid and sealed. Like a vault. For a brief instant he recalled Juell and her programming manual . . . But then he turned his full attention to the center of the room, an area that was primarily noted for its cache of multicolored pillows, all piled on the floor in a small, soft mountain.

On top of which sat Pawk Ludinder.

"The fact that you are still alive," said the angry old man, "is merely a product of my wisdom and patience. After your actions of this morning, I was advised to have you shot on sight. But I realize that you may have been prodded by ignorance. You do not yet know why you are here. Is that right?"

"It's a partial score," Chet said. "Tell me, so I can leave."

"Leave? Your humor eludes me."

"No doubt," Chet said wearily, studying the only funny face in the room.

It was hard to imagine Pawk Ludinder leading anything more than the soup line at the Salvation Army, Itpl. The tepid tyrant was no emblem of power, neither in his stature nor his clothes. Skinny, wasted, wizened, and—true to Juell's wifely words—shriveled. With not a hair on his chin or anywhere on his bony head except the faint slice of eyebrows. And the wrinkles in his skin matched those in his royal outfit; a very comfortable-looking but not elite red jacket hanging over a pair of white pants. White shoes. No insignias or medals, not even a monogram. This was Ludinder, the dictator of a whole planet, sitting cross-legged on his high stack of cushions, where just a little artwork could turn him into a toothless beggar . . . And yet there was a dire depth of cruelty in his eyes that kept Chet from being overly amused.

"You may sit down, McCoy," he was saying.

"Throw me a pillow."

"There are chairs behind you."

Chet turned—with the muscular aid of the two guards who had brought him in and now latched themselves onto his elbows—and the first thing he saw in the spot behind him was the beast of the bedroom. 830754. The huge android. Standing and staring, arms folded, head slightly out of kilter.

"My apologies, pal," Chet told him. "It came to me later that I only had one shoe to that pair. I lost the other one in a hasty exit from a startel near Vega, and her husband had it bronzed while I was heading back to Earth."

830754 groaned and barked, in cryptic binary.

Chet said, "That's not a good attitude for an android."

"Ah, you are right," was the coherent and milder reply. "I must forgive you."

"Must you?" Chet wondered.

Pawk Ludinder made it definite. "Yes, McCoy. We'll be working together for some time to come, and it'll be much easier if we are all friends. Now sit down, please."

The guards didn't act like they wanted to be friends; perhaps they weren't included in the perfect blendship. At any rate, thanks to them, Chet felt his feet leave the floor, and he was deposited in a hard chair with such force that up loomed the possibility that from then on he might *have* to sit on a pile of pillows.

But he arranged himself erectly and let his gray eyes do half the talking.

"Well, let's have it," he said. "If you can explain why a guy who has always ignored SunStop 8 as much as it can be ignored should suddenly be sitting with its latest leader in a room that looks like a zeppelin—"

"It doesn't matter what you know or think about this world or about eighters," interrupted Ludinder. "We have a great need for an Earthman bookie."

Chet sat very still.

"There must be hundreds," he protested.

The leader gazed down at him in a fatherly fashion.

"True, McCoy. But you were close at hand on SunStop 6. And you are quite well known, reasonably handsome, and at the right point between youth and maturity. Perfect qualities, wouldn't you admit? They're the exact qualities we need. Your name and picture will create a fine impression on the tickets."

"Especially if I pose in the nude."

"Your face will be enough."

"But you haven't seen the sexy scar on my belly. I found out too late that this girl from the Tager System had a diamond in her navel. What kind of tickets are you talking about?"

"Lottery tickets."

"*Lottery* tickets?" Chet repeated. "Am I supposed to be the goddamn first prize?"

"Not at all." Ludinder folded his gnarled hands on his crotch, leaning forward like a kid to a birthday cake. "McCoy," he announced slowly, "I am appointing you, officially, the Director of the SunStop 8 World Lottery."

It hit Chet with the kick of an uncushioned blastoff. He stood up, and his two guards pushed him back down; and in the interim he had time to try to put a lot of thoughts together that just didn't fit. The farther he got into this mess, he mused, the less and less sense he got out of it. Only Rocky would have the right words for the moment at hand. Rocky wasn't there to say them, but Rocky was a pal, and he wouldn't mind loaning a line for such a worthy cause.

"*What are ya,*" Chet drawled in his best imitation, "*some new kinda nut?*"

Ludinder's smile was coldly tolerant.

He said, "It's our desperation, the need to preserve the government, that makes us use you in this way. We must have a successful lottery. When my predecessor—the bearded bastard—fled to sanctuary on Earth's moon, he took the treasury with him."

"Makes it tough to meet the payroll," Chet reflected.

"True. The minor taxes we are able to impose have served to get us started." Ludinder glanced instinctively toward the du-metal doors, verifying Chet's earlier guess that it was the vault. "But our people, as you know, are fickle, and to raise the taxes would be to cut our own throats. It is the lottery that has always supported the government."

Chet nodded. "It works out in some places. All right, be my guest. Have a lottery. Have two. Let me go home and I'll teletape you a set of instructions."

"We need more than your knowledge, McCoy."

"I know, pal. My face is your fortune."

"And so it is." Ludinder hesitated thoughtfully. He interchanged cushions of red and yellow, and then, as if in need of exercise, uncrossed his legs and stretched them down the slope. At length he went on: "In the lottery that we recently completed, the prizes we paid were more than the money we collected. It's sad to admit it, especially to a foreigner, but constant revolutions on this planet have destroyed the people's confidence. Although they are accustomed to supporting lotteries, they are reluctant to risk their money with a government that may only be temporary."

"I don't blame them." Chet tried to stand up again, and this time, to his surprise, they let him stay on his feet. "Draw me a better picture," he said.

"Very well," Ludinder replied. "Chet McCoy is the new Director of the SunStop 8 World Lottery. The people do not love Earthmen, but they respect them. They've always put a lot of trust in Earth businesses; also in Earth bookies. They know that if Chet McCoy accepts their bets, he'll surely make the proper awards to the winners. They're happy again to buy lottery tickets."

"Are they? . . . Well, you know eighters better than I do," Chet said. "There's just one thing wrong. The eighters are happy. You're happy. I'm not. I don't want to be the director. I want to go back to my horse parlor in the sky."

Ludinder shook his head unblinkingly.

"Without you my government may fail. You will stay—and be comfortable and well paid."

Chet considered it. He wasn't finished with his questions, but he was through with his patience. "It can't be such a good deal. I was brought here by force—remember? Clobbered and snatched."

"That was unfortunate," Ludinder admitted. "My secret-service men were on a mission to bring back a suitable bookie by any means. Let me ask you this, McCoy—would you have come willingly if we'd asked?"

"Hell, no," Chet responded immediately.

Ludinder rested his case.

And for the first time in days, Chet was able to digest facts instead of conjectures. It seemed that he was the key to SunStop 8's salvation. It was up to him to stock the coffers, to strengthen the dictatorship, to make Ludinder's power complete and solvent. But save SunStop 8? What for? Earth was having enough trouble with the uppity planet. Relations were shattered. Rumors were flying. Invasions and sieges and boycotts and insults had already been attempted, and might someday be launched again. Save SunStop 8? God, what for? So that an underfed powergrabber could squat on his feathery throne and try to get rich enough, and strong enough, to take over all of the other SunStops?

Chet grew solemn.

"There's a group of people on Earth who for well over a century have kept bookmaking illegal. They think bookies are a special ungodly breed. They think because I live in a satellite outside of Earth's law, that

I don't give a damn about anything. They think that a bookie is a mercenary sonuvabitch who'll do anything for a buck. Well, they're wrong, pal, and so are you." He took a deep breath. He could have written a thesis on the subject and still had words left over for each and every space-chewer who tried to take him on. "So I go on fighting the law and the starcops and the Earthmen's League . . . But I wouldn't trade a single one of them for your whole lousy regime."

They were silent. Ludinder, the android, the guards; all of them silent, all of them waiting for Chet to go on. But he was quite finished. He kept his head up and waited right back at them, feeling better for the outburst, and wondering what havoc would come next.

The havoc erupted outside the room.

The sounds were frantic. Chet didn't need a decoder to sort them out as yells, pleas, and terse commands. Along with everyone else inside, he looked toward the small window in the entrance door.

Someone knocked urgently.

Ludinder gave permission.

The door opened.

It seemed that the entire eighter army was pouring into the room, but a quick census revealed a half dozen troops and a wild, ragged, middle-aged man who was being dragged on his knees. No sooner had Chet figured that out, than he himself was in escort. His two guards, reacting to some unspoken signal, hustled him out of the royal chambers and held him in the vestibule, the door closed between him and the drama. Chet could only look back through the small window and wonder.

From what he could see of the overtones and overacting, it was not going too well for the prisoner. Chet kept watching, his gray eyes shifting from person to person.

The troops gestured with clenched fists.

The captive eighter wrung his hands and whined.

Ludinder nodded. He shook his head. He nodded.

One of the soldiers gave the man a kick in the ribs. The look he got in return was more of hate than pain.

Ludinder held up a hand to the throng. They took the hint. The soldiers shut up and snapped to attention. The captive's mouth became a breathless canyon.

Shifting to another pillow, Ludinder folded his frail arms and made a great and magnificent announcement. Chet couldn't hear it, but he reasoned that it must have been in the voice of doom because it kindled the fire again.

The troops shouted and the prisoner struggled; there were blows struck and tears on the captive's face; all still going on as the confused procession clawed their way out in the same manner they had come in. Even after that, it took a while for the tumult to fade away.

And it was Chet McCoy's turn in the docket again.

"That guy sure didn't want to buy a ticket," he mentioned casually.

Ludinder shook a fist at the door. "That was another matter. The man was caught in the pantry. The guards discovered him too late and can't find the poison. Now all the food must be destroyed."

"If they can't find the poison . . ." Chet reasoned, "maybe he was just hungry."

"He would not have risked death just to fill his stomach." Ludinder gave a meaningful shrug. "No, he is an assassin. He belongs to Abraxas. Insurgents. Revolutionaries. Now there will be one less of them."

"Firing squad?"

"Yes."

"Without a trial?"

"All followers of Abraxas have already been tried in absentia and sentenced to death."

"That doesn't prove that this guy is one of them."

"He poisoned my food."

"You're not even sure of that."

"Do you expect me to eat it so that I can be sure? The man was apprehended in the pantry. He is an Abraxas bastard and he will die for it." Ludinder dismissed the issue with a wave of his hand. "Abraxas is not your concern, McCoy. You will take care of the lottery, and I will take care of the traitors."

"I've got news for you," Chet said with a firm step toward the hill of pillows. One of the guards moved swiftly to put him back in his place.

This time Chet was ready and eager. As he was about to be pounced upon, he sidestepped deftly, leaving one foot behind and adding a backhand shove that sent the guard onto a chair, draping him over the armrest by the fulcrum of his stomach.

Chet glared daringly at the other guard.

The man paled, and he lifted the blaster in fair warning that further pranks would not be taken lightly.

Chet laughed. Now that he knew his own value in Ludinder's scheme of things, he could scoff at guns that couldn't be fired. He stepped up to the blinking man, grabbed him by the uniform shirt and the crotch, and perched him on top of his bewildered comrade.

It was Chet's turn to give warning. "Make a move out of that chair and you'll have to learn to smell sideways," he told both of them, and pivoted defiantly to face Pawk Ludinder.

But he wasn't facing Ludinder. He was looking up at 830754. The hulky android was off the wall and into action and prepared to defend the throne, probably needled by his headache and longing for retaliation.

"You want to be next?" Chet asked him viciously. But his heart wasn't in it. The automaton was a little beyond the size of the two guards put together, and Chet was fresh out of antique vases. Chet swallowed his next words. It was a bookie's natural instinct to reckon the odds, whether for fights, fillies, or fiddle-dee-dee, and in this case it was clear that the odds were not to be reckoned with.

Evidently 830754 had a different viewpoint. He had probably been a bully since the first day he was activated on the assembly line, and he had no built-in qualms about slugging a guy who was only a medium-size package of flesh and blood.

"You are a nuisance," he said in a mechanical monotone.

"Flattery will get—," was all Chet had time to reply. A chain of solid, extradimensional knuckles was hurtling toward his eyes.

He ducked. It might have been a mistake. The huge fist changed course in midair and came down like an iron mallet on the back of Chet's neck. As he pitched forward, he felt the lightning cut down to his toes and bounce back to his head, and the only sensation that could penetrate the pain was the dry taste of carpeting in his mouth. He lay there paralyzed, hoping he wasn't going to get hit again.

"Stop it!" someone was saying. It must have been Ludinder. "Help him up."

He felt pressure under his armpits. Some of the straw left his mouth, and he sensed his body turning, rising . . . Finally the pain centered between his shoulders, and he was able to open his eyes.

He spread his legs to hang onto balance. His words came later from limbo.

"Never," he said absently, not even sure of what he was referring to. "Goddammit—never!" Trying desperately to clear his head, he found Ludinder's voice hanging in the spot that hurt most.

"Perhaps I didn't explain it well, McCoy," the leader was saying. "The job is far more than just your picture on the tickets. It's the whole thing. I need you to run the lottery from start to finish: to develop the system, to make it work, to promote it, to audit and follow up . . . You're the expert." He hit one hand with another. "It's got to be done!"

"Do it yourself, pal," advised Chet, still groggy.

Ludinder was being very patient. "We've arranged to make you as content as possible on SunStop 8. You will live here with us in this great building. You will be well paid in Earth dollars, a percentage of the lottery proceeds, and go back rich. And finally, to make you feel more at home, we have brought you your woman." Before Chet could think *my woman?* twice, Ludinder was talking over his shoulder. "830754, it would be best if you bring her in now."

"Yeah," Chet agreed very quietly as the android went out.

His first hazy notion was that of Juell Ludinder. He had found her in heat and left her in heat, and she would be a bang-bang way to spend the hours while he looked for starcharts of space between here and anywhere. However, he thought more soberly, it was too much to expect that Ludinder would loan out his own private eyeful for the sake of the lottery . . . From Earth then, and who would it be? Dear Dinya of the lovelorn tapes? The safecracking Elizabeth? Bonnie, the most female bookie? *Who?* He didn't want any of them. He'd have his hands full just getting himself off this wonderplanet, and escaping for two would be double trouble.

The door opened and closed.

The girl in 830754's arms didn't come easily. She was stomping on the android's feet and jamming her elbows into his ribs. Her eyes flamed brighter than her hair.

Chet stood stunned.

Not Juell. Not any girl he knew from Earth. And not at all a girl who by any stretch of logic could be called *his woman.*

"Damn you, Chet!" she yelled, as bitter as moon beer. "What the hell are you up to?"

For once he couldn't find an answer.

Avon Clahr. The redhead from the SaunArena. The stacked beauty who knew all about SunStop 8; she hated it, feared it, and ran away from all contact with it. Now right in the middle of the eighters.

Avon. Of all people.

6.
A Word from Abraxas

"You can go straight to hell," she said. "You—you said you weren't involved in eighter affairs."

In place of the silvon du-suit that he remembered so well, she was wearing a looser outfit of yellow disposies; but, just as before, she consumed Chet's interest.

It was strange what a deep impression she had made on him in the one time she had crossed his path. He now realized that he knew little about her. Once he had touched her in the high flying mist, and once he had talked to her on the floor of the arena, when she had tried to warn him about all this. But she had never identified herself as more than a sixer who worked for the Towers; his feeling of closeness to this full-figured, red-haired girl with blazing green eyes was based on nothing but intuition. And yet, even while his brain had been put upon to deal with his kidnappers, her image had never been very far from his mind.

The sight of her in that room, the one touch of color and brightness in the grim circle of Ludinder's men, reminded Chet of why he had chased after her in the first place. To see her again gave him a moment of pleasure for which there was no logical explanation, followed by a throb of pain that reflected his guilt. Her face told him much more: a fear to which he could relate gleamed under her surge of anger.

"They picked me out of thin air," Chet explained.

"Then they assumed from our meeting in the Saun-Arena that you were mine. Tyranny knows no bounds."

She frowned. "And what am I mixed up in?"

"I haven't measured it yet. Let's find out right now." He turned to Ludinder. "To get back to the subject, pal . . . we were talking about a lottery that I'm *not* going to run. Are you going to make me more offers? Don't bother. There's no price—I'm just not booking this event. I'm going back where I came from, and you can grind your goddamn lottery into stardust."

Ludinder's face hardened.

"Are you finished?" he asked.

"No, one more thing," Chet added indignantly. "Tell 830754 to quit feeling up my woman."

The android stiffened at the mention of his grasp on Avon. Slowly, he uncoiled his arm from under her breasts and looked innocently at his leader. Avon whirled free, prepared to slap his face, but it was too high up. She clenched her fist for an anxious moment, then turned and walked to Chet.

He took her hand. He didn't expect that he'd been forgiven, but when it came to taking sides, she was not likely to chum around with the eighters. Having her on his side was the best thing that had happened to him on SunStop 8.

Ludinder was saying, "I advise you to reconsider, McCoy."

"Why should I?" Chet said. "Let him get his own girl."

Ludinder squeezed the corner of a pillow.

"I'm not talking about 830754. I'm talking about you." His voice grew malicious. "McCoy, I'm asking you one last time to take care of the lottery for me." He held up a hand. "Before you answer, let me warn you that the alternative is not pleasant. The prisons have ruined many a man."

"And you're a living example," Chet noted.

"That's true. During the period of our uprising, I was confined for more than three years. But I eventually escaped to lead the final victories." He changed suddenly to drier words. "But your situation is different, McCoy."

Chet felt the weight of the jailhouse threat. All through his illegal career he had managed, sometimes by the most intricate means, to avoid spending even a single day in a bread-and-water building, and to not even think about the hot prisons on Mercury. But now, in innocence, he seemed to be heading for a cell.

Or was Ludinder bluffing?

Chet called it. "You don't have the guts to throw an Earthman in jail without a charge. Not unless you're looking for an all-out space war, and I doubt that your little wonderplanet is ready for that."

"There is a charge," Ludinder replied matter-of-factly. "A serious charge."

"What—slugging a few of your boys?"

"No, McCoy. Much more than that. You've violated a basic interstellar law." Ludinder bared a stony smile. "Illegal entry, of course."

Chet raised his eyebrows. He began to understand the determination of his abductor, and he began to see the importance of the role he was supposed to play. Overnight he had been flung onto a pinnacle where he would become the rallying point of the eighters and the banner of a firm government. He had not thought in his years of taking bets that the bookie business could support or topple the throne of a political dictator. *And yet . . .*

"Illegal!" he protested. "I was kidnapped!"

"That you'll never prove. No, McCoy, you're here without a passport, without a visa, and with no record of having passed through any legitimate port of entry." Ludinder let it sink in. "The sentence for illegal entry is practically automatic," he continued impersonally. "One year in prison, and then deportation back to Earth."

"A year?" Chet repeated, mostly to himself.

Ludinder nodded. "It's the equivalent of an Earth year, minus seventeen days. Coincidentally, it's about the same amount of time you would be required to stay to conduct the lottery."

The old leader's offered choice balanced precariously in Chet's mind. A year on SunStop 8. *And where did he want to spend it?* In this fine castle of a building, or in jail. In chains either way. He felt Avon's hand tighten on his own, and it prompted a question.

"What about her?"

"She also entered illegally," Ludinder answered, and let it go at that.

Chet was aware of the implications. He looked at Avon, and he knew what she wanted. She didn't want jail. He looked back at the skinny figure on top of the pillows. Ludinder didn't want jail, either; he wanted first aid; he wanted an infamous bookie to put glue on his government seat. Avon, Ludinder, 830754, and the two guards: all of them waiting for Chet's decision, and all of them sure of what it would be, because the luxury of the capitol had a big edge over the confinement of a prison. But the edge was merely physical. Emotionally it was another matter; a thing that none of them could have put into words. Chet knew it had something to do with not helping your enemies, not conforming to an eighter mold, not selling out to a threat . . . But whether or not he acknowledged those feelings, the more active stream of his mind was concerned with something else: the best way to take his leave. Juell had advised him—with musical accompaniment—that he could never get out of the capitol building alive. From his own tour of the premises, remembering the doors and the fences and the gates and the heavy patrols, he had to agree with her. He didn't know if it would be any easier to escape from the jail. Probably not. But he had to see it to find out.

And then, as if by invitation, Pawk Ludinder's voice crossed over his thoughts and brought him right up to the $100 window.

"You've heard all I've got to say, McCoy. There are only two ways out for you—the lottery or prison. You can think again if you like."

"I've done all the thinking I can," Chet replied firmly. "And I'm not going to do it, pal. No lottery for me."

There was a pause of ten seconds, then sounds rose behind him. He didn't have to look to know what was happening. The android and the guards were moving closer in anticipation of the order to come.

It came as he expected: a terse command with an undertone of ominous tolerance, suggesting that this episode of insubordination was not the end of the game, but only the beginning.

"Take them," said Ludinder.

And that was that.

It occurred to Chet McCoy as he sat in the tail section of the military soarer that he and Avon might be the sole representatives of the tourist trade on SunStop 8. From their low-flying position, he could see defunct casinos and amusement areas all around Decatur, and he could imagine them in their prime, all lighted up, noisy, with the action of free-wheeling crowds within and about them. Now, scattered below the soarer, these bare structures were covered by webbing, slim plastic protection that might or might not keep them from rotting until the recovery of the wonderplanet. The parking fields around these former havens of joy were completely empty, where once they held thousands of airborne soarers and as many jitters that came by land. And just as empty were the huge pod areas that no longer accepted the daily and nightly flights of rich and hell-for-leather visitors from the other SunStops. Not much left of it, Chet thought. The eighter world, the outer planet of the miracle loop, once proud host to the galaxy, was broke and struggling and void.

But not dead. Not quite dead.

Its unique soarers still flew through dazzling blue skies, powered by the rays of the double star. When both suns were up, as they were now, the soarer operated at maximum speed and maneuverability. With one sun in view, it flew more slowly, but measured up to any traveler's standards. At night, with both power sources gone, it relied on stored energy which powered it through the air at the pace of a fiver snail, but this was a small planet and haste was generally no factor.

And on the ground—Chet could see some movement on the roads—were jitters: the small open cars that were so popular on the SunStops, and that relied for locomotion on the same pair of healthy suns. Fast on two, medium on one, slow in the dark.

Slow in the dark, Chet thought again.

Like a laugh.

What all this meant to him was that because of the brightness of the day they were going to get to the prison in quick order. He wasn't anxious to get there, but since it seemed inevitable, he was already looking at it as his next starting point for escape; and on the basis of that, he was glad they were moving along at full speed.

Avon saw it differently.

"You don't seem to be worrying much about it," she was saying. The way she was wedged side-by-side with him in the rear section of the soarer had them both facing their old friend from the royal chambers, 830754, who was there to make sure they didn't move. "You could get into that prison and never get out. Living on six, I've heard plenty about a lot of lost souls.

Honestly, Chet, you could have handled the lottery."

"I suppose so, honey," he replied, still in deep thought. "Let's wait and see how it goes."

In the facing seat, the android expanded his shoulders like the twin cliffs of Titan. "I can tell you how it will go, McCoy. In a few days you will be begging to return. You are too accustomed to the good life. There is none of it where you are going."

Chet smiled. "In a few days, pal, I'll have the warden betting on soarer polo . . . and winning!"

"This is not Earth," the android advised, then turned quickly as the pilot yelled.

The shout was loud enough to bring all of the eighters to their feet. Besides the pilot and 830754, there were four others in the soarer crew, and three uniformed soldiers who were Chet's official escorts, and they were all looking or hurrying to the front of the soarer to find out what was happening.

Chet strained to see. *What were these goddamn space-chewers up to?*

The heavy bar across his stomach prevented him from leaving his seat, but through the scrambling heads and bodies he found a view of the front windshield; and what he saw took a few moments to figure out.

Coming at them, and very close, a pair of soarers.

In flight between the two oncoming soarers, one end attached to each, was an opaque sheet of some black fabric. The dark sheet was about five times the width and length of Chet's soarer; and he knew what it was even a second before the pilot's frantic explanation.

"They're trying to block the light!"

"Get us out of the way," instructed 830754 with authority. "Take a blast at them." Grabbing the teletransmitter, he began sending a distress call, filling it in with brief descriptions of the problem.

Meanwhile, the two enemy soarers were almost on

top of them. The black shield was already casting a shadow. And worse than that, Chet now saw the scurrying images of other soarers all around them. . .

The government soarer got off one blast before the power went down the dark drain . . . it missed everything.

And then all bright light left the soarer. The cover was overhead, matching their flight path and their pace. Enough indirect light came in from the edges to let Chet see what was going on inside, but he was more concerned about what was going on outside.

The attackers were buzzing around under full solar power, but the government ship was barely moving and losing altitude every second.

Chet wished he could move. Sitting still in that situation was a Jovian torture far beyond the pain of Avon's fingernails digging into his arm.

"Chet, for God's sake—what is it?" she moaned.

He squeezed his hands on the bar that held them in their seats. "Someone doesn't want us to go to jail," he said. "And I don't know if that's good or bad." The bar wouldn't budge. He was still trapped in the back, helpless.

He could only watch.

The first laser silently pierced the midsection of the soarer, missing everything within but leaving the gaping evidence of a hole in each side. Up front, the android added those facts to his continuous low-beam communications.

"They are firing at us," he reported evenly. "But no blasts—they are only lasers." He went on to estimate the number of enemy ships that were in the air.

The second beam of laser light came in across the bow, destroying part of the windshield and the co-seat in the cockpit. The soldier who was sitting there was killed instantly; and 830754, who was leaning over the seats to use the communicator, barely escaped with his du-skin intact.

They were still losing altitude.

Settling with them were the two ships that carried and guided the blotter sail that absorbed all the power. The silent flights of their companion ships continued to pop in and out of Chet's view.

A third shot of narrow light burst through the lower front of the soarer, angling up to where it caught another soldier in the throat, and passed on through him to its exit above the side window. The soldier fell dead. No blood—the wound was cauterized. The lasers were taking their toll, but, as bad as it was, Chet was still grateful that no blasters were being used. One hit from a ship-size blaster could have wiped them all out in an instant.

As it did to the soarer on his right.

Chet had been looking out the window at it, trying to anticipate the aim of its next laser shot, when suddenly it exploded in midair and the pieces fell away in red bursts of fire.

Up front, the android stopped broadcasting.

"We have got them now!" he thundered, and came stamping down the aisle toward Chet and Avon. He raised a fist. "Octo, McCoy. Our air force is here, and you will see the end of the fools who think they can attack us right over Decatur. It will be sweet and short. They have no blasters."

The opaque screen that had been covering them tilted to let in the sunlight, as the soarer on the left was destroyed moments after its partner. And then the screen itself was blasted into small pieces before it could touch the government ship. Now Chet had a full look at the sky, and it was not as serene as it was once advertised to be.

He had not realized how many soarers were involved in the battle. Now that he could see, he could not attempt to count them. He couldn't even count the ones that were going down. The lasers of the attacking ships were no match for the blasters of those who flew for Ludinder, and evidently the enemy had no blasters of their own. They were outgunned and far outnumbered. Each one, in its turn, gave in to a dark explosion and disappeared from the sky, leaving smoke that drifted like storm clouds on Earth.

And Chet, still struggling to get loose of the bar in his lap, saw it through to the end, making no contribution to either cause, and not sure what he would have done if he could have gotten free.

He felt a slight jolt in his ribs as the soarer landed in one of the large parking areas around an abandoned casino. A few other government ships were coming down in the same vicinity, and the wreckage of many enemy soarers were in plain sight in every direction, burning and melting to their last ash.

The android pressed a stud that released the bar holding Chet and Avon. "We are going to go the rest of the way—not far—in a land jitter. They will not be expecting it, so they will not have time to plan a different attack."

Helping Avon up, Chet moved with her out of the soarer. He stretched the stiffness out of his arms and legs, while staring at the wreckage around him. Now he could see the bodies of the men who had flown in the other ships, and they were eighters of all ages, clothed in various outfits of rugged outdoor style, nothing very official. Except dead. They were all officially dead.

Chet looked back at the android.

"Who are they?"

"Ah, they *were* men of Abraxas," replied 830754.

"Abraxas? Like the guy they found poisoning the food?"

"The same, yes. Fools who never learn. They have little to fight with—you saw, lasers against blasters. The few soarers they had were stolen from an unprotected field of a local shooting club. Other than that . . ." The android seized Chet's arm and led him to an open jitter. Avon followed in the grasp of a uniformed guard. When they were seated, 830754 went on: "They cannot put us down. But still they keep fighting—why? Ah, it is the power of Abraxas. He is like a god to them."

Chet took another glance at the parking field.

"That bunch might disagree with you," he said. "They didn't get much godlike protection. You ran up a big score."

830754 shrugged. "It makes no difference. If they had been captured, they would have been executed immediately. Dead one way or the other."

As Chet started to give it some thought, Avon roared into the conversational gap. He had seen anger in her eyes before, but now they showed the pain and pressure of the long, surprising day.

"It's *your* fault, Chet," she said. "Every one of those dead men back there—*your* fault. You keep taking other people's lives and twisting them to your own screwed-off ways. I just hope to hell—"

"Wait a minute, honey," Chet interrupted. "I'm not taking credit for any of it. Those guys who attacked us didn't care if I was Chet McCoy or Johnny Pumpkin. They only cared about what I was supposed to do, and they wanted me out of the way, dead or alive. Tell her, pal."

The android put his gears into a shrug.

"Seems so," he agreed. "Abraxas will usually fight us for any reason. His followers look for reasons, big or small. Today it was special. However, they did not come to kidnap the Earthman bookie . . . They came to stop the lottery."

"Which brings up a point," Chet said. "How does Abraxas know about me? How does he know that I'm here, or who I am? And how does he know that I'm on my way to the goddamn jail?"

The jitter hit a bump. When it settled again, 830754 was ready to answer Chet's questions.

He said, "Either Abraxas is able to read our minds, or there is a traitor in the capitol."

"What do you think?" Chet prompted.

"One is as inconceivable as the other."

"Why? Traitors are nothing new."

"Ah, but a spy who has no limits. Who knows our every move, and even our thoughts."

Chet nodded. "You've got a problem, pal."

He turned to Avon, and she had a problem, too. She was slumped in the seat.

"The hell with eighters," she stammered. "I want to get out of here."

Chet looked her straight in the eye, and reached out a hand to touch her red hair.

"I'll figure out something," he said softly.

Then he heard gravel grinding under the jitter's tires, and his attention drifted to the two-story building that looked as if it had been the first piece of construction on SunStop 8. Old in style and materials. Junky, he decided. Barred windows and high turrets and the afternoon patrol. A few gaunt faces peering down from inside. The looping eight on a weather-worn flag. Another flag, in better condition. A strangely-bred dog throwing up at the base of a square yellow sign. The sign said something about Ludinder and a speed zone. An alert group of soldiers waiting at the main entrance, waiting at the bottom of eight wide steps . . . waiting for the Earthman and his bride.

Cozy.

Real cozy.

Shit.

Part Two

CHET McCOY GOES IN AND OUT OF JAIL . . . AND ROCKY TAKES A SWING

8
SHIFFMAN 77

7.
A Clink in the Pod Chamber

It wasn't that Rocky had an ear for the rest of the world when he was involved in affairs of the heart, but many anxious days in orbit had set him up for certain awaited messages; so that even though his bed partner was a sound barrier by herself, some deep and expectant resonance enabled him to hear the familiar sound of du-steel against du-steel.

He opened his eyes.

He let the sound penetrate his mind and be absorbed. At first he thought that something had broken under the weight of the bed. But that wasn't it. It was a clink in the pod chamber. No doubt about it. Someone had arrived on *Ruffian*. Someone had entered the satellite. And he *knew* who it had to be.

In his excitement he shook Brauna's breast . . . And she, taking it seriously, stuck her tongue in his mouth, which made it impossible for him to talk until he blew it out with a huff.

Then he said, "Listen, listen—"

"*Echoes sound afar,*" she hummed dreamily.

"No!" said Rocky, breaking away. "It's Chet! He's back. He's home. That's why he ain't answered any of my calls. He's been coming home."

"Good for him," was Brauna's sleepy reply. But Rocky was already out of the bed and yanking at her arm.

"C'mon, doll. We've gotta say hello. I'll bet he

brought me back a case of boozer pills, and we can have a party. A big welcome party."

"I don't feel like going to a party. I'm sore all over."

"That ain't nothing not to go to a party for."

"It is to me."

"Huh?"

She turned over onto her stomach. "Call me when the guests arrive."

Rocky clenched a fist, and then he shrugged. Let her be, he thought. This was no time to argue. With a yell, he ran naked from the bedroom compartment to the control room.

And there, coming to a stop, he closed his mouth.

Aside from a small portable scanner that was rolling around on the floor by the console, the control room was empty of people and foreign objects. He watched the scanner settle down in diminishing circles. It was a silent act, and it lent weight to Rocky's inner argument that the scanner by itself could not have produced the clink in the pod chamber.

And secondly–Chet didn't carry a scanner.

The Rock began to scratch his hairy stomach, searching for the right conclusion . . .

Someone was on *Ruffian.*

Someone who wasn't Chet McCoy.

And someone, judging from the position of the scanner, who was hiding behind the console in the control room.

"C'mon out, you goddamn space-chewer," Rocky snorted. "If I have to come get you, you're gonna get bashed in the balls."

"I was just looking for my scanner," a man's voice responded.

"Like hell. You lost it when you went to hide."

A short, pudgy man in a light pod outfit popped up from behind the console.

"Have you seen it?" he asked.

"Yeah." Rocky pointed to the floor.

The man moved around the console. He picked up the scanner, dusted it with his hand, blew on it, and put it into the tool kit that was attached to his waistband. When he looked again at Rocky, it was with a double and belligerent chin.

"Where's McCoy?" he snapped.

"Huh?" said Rocky.

"Chet McCoy. Your boss. Where is he?"

"I don't know."

"Don't give me that stuff."

"Huh?"

"I know he's here."

"Huh?"

"I want answers, not sound effects!"

But Rocky wasn't even hearing the questions. He was studying the face that was sticking out of the pod suit: the red, chubby cheeks and the small, round eyes . . . And he was trying to put it all together and place it where it belonged. He couldn't make it fit.

Suddenly, he snapped his fingers.

"You ain't a starcop," he said decisively.

"Of course I'm not," replied the intruder, seemingly anxious to clarify the point. "My name is Stin Breed, and I'm from the Bright Day Collection Division. And you might as well know that I'm the best skip-tracer in the business. Through me, my company's recovered a fortune in bad debts. I'd be a field manager by now, except that they need me so much for the real thing. They know how good I am."

Rocky couldn't have cared less. He left the control room to put on his white shorts; and by the time he returned, he had missed out on the last part of Stin Breed's speech and mid-year resolutions, and was none the worse for it.

"So what are you sneaking around here for?" he wanted to know.

"Just doing my job," replied Breed.

"Huh?"

"Collecting bad debts."

The Rock considered the occupation with his usual open mind.

He said, "Well, all right, Breed. We've got a welcher who owes us a few thousand superbucks since June of 2057.3. Plenty of times I was gonna go bash him till we got it, but Chet never let me. He always says—"

"I'm not here for a solicitation," Breed stated firmly.

"Huh?"

"I came to collect—*right here.* McCoy is delinquent."

"He's thirty-four years old!"

"Then he's old enough to know better," Breed said. He hooked his fat thumbs in his waistband. "In case you don't know, Chet McCoy skipped out of the Towers, bag and baggage, and he left a bill of . . ." Breed picked a computer minicard out of his tool kit and turned it over to see the score, ". . . 3,712 superdollars. That includes the AmDrive, the room, the meals, the laundry, the bar bill, and everything else he signed for including a night at the SaunArena."

The teeth that bared in mean defiance belonged to Rocky.

"You're lying. Chet ain't a welcher."

"Why not? He's everything else," was Breed's opinion. "He's a bookie and an outlaw. He has this place orbiting where the starcops can't get him. He's got . . . But I'm just wasting time with you. Tell him I'm here, and tell him I'm waiting for the money."

"Who?" asked Rocky.

"McCoy."

"He ain't here."

"There's no use covering up for him. He had his vacation—a *free* vacation, I might add—and then he ran home, straight back here, because he's got a business to take care of. So don't try any fancy stories. I've got Chet McCoy figured to a T."

"I told you, he ain't here."

"Then you won't mind if I see for myself."

The Rock minded. He would have preferred to break the intruder's head; but Chet was always warning him about committing violence without due provocation, whatever that meant.

"Well?" Breed was saying.

"Go ahead and look," Rocky conceded, deciding on peaceful and patient methods, and determining with some mental flashbacks that he had nothing to hide. But he wasn't going to be an usher. He sat at the console, swung his legs up onto the light panel, rubbed his chin, straightened his shorts, and waited for Stin Breed to make the rounds. . .

The roly-poly collector waddled into bedroom number one—Chet McCoy's compartment. The bed was tightly made, the closet was partially empty, the drawers held a small supply of disposies, and both the newstape and music players were set in the OFF position. There were no current signs of life. Undaunted, Breed walked into the adjoining bathroom; and that also would have been a wasted trip except that he spent about thirty seconds using the facilities. Then he was ready for the big push. For a short while he stared at the door on the opposite side of the bathroom, mulling on its possibilities. Obviously it led to another bedroom. Obviously Chet McCoy was hiding in that bedroom. All other areas had already been searched.

Stin Breed reached for the stud. And as the door slid open soundlessly, he ran like a bull into bedroom number two. . .

Brauna had been dozing in a welcome interlude.

The sudden noise was startling enough by itself, but the charge of the red-faced man in the pod suit with the bouncing tool kit was a sight that dug icy needles into her spine; for her immediate and only thought was that he'd come for a belated rescue in answer to her fanciful teletransmissions. She didn't know the exact penalty for a false alarm, but she knew that she was guilty. And she knew that her only chance was to convince the excited lawman that her calls had been real pleas for help. She had to carry on.

She jumped to her feet, but not to the floor. Standing naked on the mattress, she spread her hands and yelled to the high heavens—

"Rape! Rape! Help me, I've been raped! Please help me! I'm sore all over! I've been raped and raped and raped!"

"What the hell—?" Breed stammered, just before Rocky dashed into the compartment and grabbed him by the suit's seal at the collar.

"Keep your goddamn hands off my broad," the Rock stormed.

"I haven't touched her," Breed insisted, but Rocky pulled him closer and glared into his eyes.

"What are you collecting, buddy? You're some sonuvabitch, sneaking and screwing all over the place."

"But—"

"She's my broad, and I ain't giving out samples."

"But I didn't rape her."

The Rock turned to the girl. "Have you been raped?"

"Dozens of times," Brauna said wearily.

"Huh?"

"Oh, thirty or forty times, I guess."

"She's a liar!" Stin Breed shouted.

Rocky stared him down. "You been counting?"

"No, no. I just mean that I didn't rape her dozens of times."

"Once is plenty enough," the Rock said scoldingly. He tightened his grip on Breed's collar and pinned the man against the wall. "You ain't had a Bright Day after all, buddy," he went on. "No matter what Chet says about it, I'm gonna bash you."

"You better not," said Breed. "You wouldn't dare."

"How come?"

"Because of my position. I'm an authorized–"

It was the end of the conversation.

The uppercut came from down around Rocky's knees, and by the time it arrived at Breed's soft chin, it had gathered more than twenty-nine years of Wiggeneer plasma, more than enough fuel to lift Breed's feet off the floor. He came down in a heap as Rocky stepped out of the way. The scanner fell out of the tool kit again and rolled under the bed. Rocky went after it.

When the scanner and its unconscious owner were deposited in their pod and exiled to a nearby asteroid known only to Rocky's secret soul, Rocky returned to the control room to activate the terminal. Then, once his AmDrive reservation was confirmed, he went back to his compartment to pack a bag.

"What about me?" Brauna inquired, watching him.

"Huh?"

"That starcop will be back with the troops. If you're getting out, so am I."

Rocky shook his head.

"No, doll. That ain't a cop, and I ain't taking it on the lam." He tucked in a white overshirt. He sealed his belt. "I've gotta go to SunStop 6. Chet wouldn't cheat nobody out of a hotel bill or anything else. Sure as hell, he's in trouble. And, doll, when he's in trouble, he needs his old buddy, Rocky."

There were tears in her eyes. "What'll I do while you're gone?"

"Just stick around. Take a rest. You're always hollering about being sore, anyhow."

"I don't really . . . really . . ." She buried her face in the pillow.

The Rock sniffed in sympathy, but went on dressing and packing; and when he was done, he turned to say good-bye to her. She was still lying face down on the bed. To her credit, the blending of curves was enticing from any angle.

And saying good-bye, Rocky thought gingerly, was no way to say good-bye . . .

8.
A Time Slot

830754 pulled open the barred door, and Chet went on in.

The cell was no more or less than he'd imagined it; fitting the guess he'd made outside that this was the oldest building on the SunStops. The room was bleak and gray. Overhead was a dim panel of solar light that was set in behind a protective cage. On one wall was the only window, small and barred. On the other wall was a faucet that had lost its sink and pointed instead to a drain in the concrete floor. And at various points in Chet's sight were his cellmates—three of them—who dug their elbows into their cots and lifted their heads to look at him.

"This is McCoy—an Earthman," the android announced. And after he closed the door he added: "You will not like it here, McCoy."

Chet touched the nearest wall. "Well, it's a lot cooler than the domes on Mercury."

The comparison was lost on the eighters in the cell. No one sat up to take notice. One of the prisoners spread his elbows and went to sleep. The other two just continued to look on with no change in expression. Already Chet could sense an environment of gloom, and boredom and claustrophobia, like a doctor's waiting room. Darkly.

Cursing and kicking her captors, Avon had been taken away. Up the chute. Evidently the women prisoners—Chet didn't know how many—were kept in a segregated area on the second floor. Chet raised his eyes to the ceiling. Every prisoner, he decided, probably gave his first thoughts to sex. A year in this place without a woman? Never.

His eyes came level again.

"Is there anyway to get out on weekends?" he asked frivolously, and 830754 answered from the better side of the bars.

"You could get out right now with a promise to cooperate. That is all you need."

"Uh-uh," said Chet. "That's all *you* need."

"We can get another bookie from Earth."

Chet smiled. "If you think you can . . . You were just lucky to find me on SunStop 6. Try to kidnap somebody from Earth itself and you're going to find our whole space navy on your back. You know what that means, pal. They'll pull the plug and let your little planet sink slowly into the double sunset."

"Ah, then you will be here to sink with us." The android wrapped both of his large hands around the bars that separated him from Chet. "I will not be coming back, McCoy. When you have had enough of the prison, notify any of the guards. If it is not too late—if we have not found another man for the lottery—then *maybe* Ludinder will listen to your pleas."

"Have him hold his breath," Chet advised, but there was no reply.

830754 was gone.

The doors were closed and locked.

The light was bad. The small room was overcrowded. And Chet wasn't used to the smell of the unwashed eighters. None of the three seemed very sociable; not a word came as Chet looked around at each of them. The man in the upper cot was much older than the two men below, but all three had beards. It was one of the younger men that was sleeping. The others were awake but noncommittal.

Walking between them, Chet ignored the empty cot

on the higher level and sat on the floor instead, leaning his back against the rough texture of the far wall, with the patch of window letting in a remnant of daylight far above his head. He brought his knees up toward his chest. He rested his arms.

A damned spacehole.

An escape, if even possible, was going to take plenty of patience and planning, as well as time and knowledge. Not to mention luck. *And help from these goddamn eighters.*

None of whom had spoken a single word in his presence.

Chet gave them a glance. "Are you guys alive?"

Above him, the old man stirred. He put his mostly white beard over the edge of the cot and studied Chet from one end to the other. Finally he shook his head.

"They took your watch," he said disappointedly. His voice tended to crack on the consonants.

"I don't have a watch," Chet replied.

"Too bad, then." The man pulled his beard away.

"But I don't need one," Chet went on. "I have an implant." It was not uncommon, despite the expense and the initial discomfort, for a bookie to get a time implant. For one who takes bets on everything in the universe, the vital factor is knowing when any event is taking place in spacewhere. The business is based on time. It is necessary to record the exact time when a bet is taken, and to compare it to the relative spacetime of the thing that's being bet on. Otherwise, conniving bettors tend to pick winners *after* the event has occurred. In other events, like the freefalls, the payoffs are made on timed results, where sometimes just a few seconds separates the win, place, and show . . . And with Chet, all of these intricate clock calculations came automatically from within his mind.

For that reason, he suddenly found himself to be the most popular man in the cellblock.

"I don't know what time it is here," he had to explain. "I'm still mentally adjusted to the sixer planet. What's the time base on SunStop 8?"

The old man didn't know. Neither did the other two. But in whispers they passed the word down the row of cells until they found someone with the answer.

"It's 1.3066," relayed the old man. "Now you've got the base. So what time is it?"

Chet held up a hand. "Give me a chance, pal." Then he let the local base number enter the register of his mind, and he could almost feel the clicks of the automatic adjustment, although he knew that there were really no clicks. The implanted microchip was programmed to reset electronically from the energy impulses of the brain in the same way that it came up with the exact time whenever it sensed a mental request. The whole thing was just a modified version of the time-of-day clock in a computer.

Everyone was waiting for its results.

Chet put down his hand. He was ready. *But why were they all so interested?*

Finally he told them: "Exactly 1618. Late in a warm eighter afternoon."

His cellmates looked at each other and nodded. One of the younger men went to the cell door and passed the word along. Then he went back to his cot and just sat there.

The return to silence was not what Chet had expected. He tried a few questions, but got no answers. It was irritating. The excitement over the correct time seemed to have subsided as abruptly as it had begun, as if they had only been testing his ability to do it. But he thought that the present circumstances made it a useless talent. In a place like this, it was better to forget about time.

He tried it. Back to the wall, he blanked out the implant and dozed.

It was dark when he woke up.

His first thoughts were of yesterday's women. Avon, a sixer who coolly loathed him, was somewhere in the prison, up above. Juell, an eighter who hotly tempted him, was probably with her husband in the royal suite. They both haunted him. Avon the most. Avon hadn't done a damn thing to cause her punishment. It was a rough deal for her.

For her sake as well as his own initial reaction to being locked up, he might have called it quits right then, right from his spot on the hard floor; but he had a sensation that he had felt a few times before in a life full of sensations—something was going to happen. It wasn't based entirely on intuition. It was partly based, once again, on his time implant.

As the night continued, Chet began to get the attention he had so briefly received during the afternoon. The three men in the room approached him at various intervals, quietly asking the time, and then relaying the information to all the others on the lower floor. As midnight passed, they checked more often. In every cell, every man seemed to be asleep, but not a single one really was; all were waiting furtively for Chet's mind to add up the ticks. He waited with them. He didn't know why. His status as the center of the prison universe was of no help in charting the course of things to come. All he could do was tell time. Like a paid computer. *Good evening and welcome to the central info bank, reads the display. The correct time for area eight is exactly . . .*

0115.

One of the men climbed out of his lower berth and took a seat on the floor close to Chet.

0119.

The other young man left his cot and walked to the cell door.

0123.

The old man sat above them all, touching his white

beard and making other silent motions that Chet couldn't understand.

0127.

Chet announced it under his breath. The man next to him nodded and held up three fingers. The man at the door stuck his arm out between the bars and held up three fingers.

0128.

There was furtive movement everywhere. Chet's cellmates motioned him away from his usual spot. He stood up.

0129.

Everyone crawled under the lower bunks and covered their ears. Chet rolled in alongside the man whose prison odor was the worst of the group, but the smell was overshadowed by the musk of excitement.

0130.

The wall blew up.

The entire wall at their end of the building. Without a sound, it blew—up or down, or in or out—he couldn't tell. Silently, it exploded or imploded. Then the noise came as the structure splintered, crashed, collapsed, powdered, and dissolved—the blastprints of a laser cannon. And a thick cloud of smoke rolled in.

Chet raced his companions to the cell door. He hung there on the bars, just one of many watching, pushing to see, straining at the leash.

Before the smoke cleared, the army came through it.

Chet had seen them before in the wreckage of the attacking soarers. Rebels of Abraxas. Revolutionary digits of SunStop 8. A haphazard army, with their dirty clothes and bouncing laserods stuck in their belts. Coming on like the tail of a comet behind the cannon's demolition . . . Hundreds of them and hundreds of strong voices, running into the cellblock and spreading to cover every centimeter of it. Born in the smoke, and now they were fire. No one tried to stop them. The only sign of government resistance was the wail of a very loud siren. Wherever the guards were, they were too smart for suicide. The rebels were temporarily but absolutely in command.

Short beams from the laserods quickly cut away the door locks. The cells emptied and the army doubled in size. Chet was swept up and onward in a wave of moving, shouting men, an unarmed segment of the roaring jailbreak.

He joined the group that gathered at the chute to the upper floor. Pushing his way to the front, he managed to get into the next load and rose full speed to the exit above. As he raced down the aisle searching for Avon, cell doors were being cut open and women in prison clothes were pouring out to block his path. Weaving through them, shoving them aside, he went on looking for the head of red hair. When he suddenly found her, he stopped and caught his breath.

Her cell door was melted and wide open. She wasn't walking through it.

"You can't stay here, honey," he told her hurriedly. "I'm getting out with Abraxas and then I'm going back to Earth. Without me you could be stuck here for the whole year. This is our chance."

"Take it yourself, Chet," she said. She was standing at the far wall with her arms tightly folded. In the drab gray of the prison uniform she seemed tougher and more determined than ever. "Your tracks always lead someplace beyond hell. I don't care what you jump into this time, but once and for all, damn you, leave me out of it!"

He looked behind him. The second floor was emptying out. There was little time for joining the exodus. There was no time for holding court or offering incentives. If they didn't get away with the rest of the rebel army . . . He stepped toward Avon.

"You'll go willingly or unconsciously—but you'll go."

"No. And don't touch me."

"That's not the right attitude," he said, moving closer. "This is all for your own good."

"I'll scream to hell and back."

"Go ahead. It'll add to the festivities."

She screamed.

He put his hands on her waist and lifted her high; and slung her over his shoulder . . .

The last of the rebels were leaving the courtyard when Chet came down the front steps. As he started to run after them, he saw the guards come out of hiding. Dozens of jailers, together and regrouped, were rounding the corner of the building, anxious to save what face they could. And Chet observed rather unhappily that he and his wiggly red-haired burden were the only victims in their range. Quickly he looked both ways and judged the distances. Between himself and the guards; between himself and the fleeing followers of Abraxas . . . He decided without any more hesitation that the delay to get Avon had cost him his chance for freedom. The guards would be on him before he could get anywhere near the rebel army.

He set Avon on her feet and gripped her shoulders. "Get out of here," he shouted above the reverberations of the rooftop siren; and when she started to shake her head, he shook her like a stern father. "You can make it, but you've got to run."

Her lips moved without a sound. If there were words spoken, they were under the siren's noise.

"Get going!" he urged again. He turned her around and slapped her hard on the ass to get her started. Over her shoulder, she looked back at him strangely. The lively eyes that usually flashed with vim and vigor were mostly soft and frightened and undecided; until at last she turned her head and ran in the direction of the other escapees. Chet watched her go, wondering if he'd ever see her again, and realizing how much he wanted to.

He moved to meet the onrushing guards. They'd never catch up to Avon, he told himself, because he was going to take care of them. All twenty . . . thirty . . . forty of them. "Just remember," he yelled, "that Ludinder wants to keep me *alive*!"

The siren took away his words and roared splittingly through his head. But he had to think anyway. The guards were closing and charging. Chet took a deep breath. Then he drew a straight line in the dirt in front of him, using the toe of his right shoe. Stepping back, he pointed down to the line like Moses dividing the sea.

Sure enough the guards stopped momentarily on the other side of the line. A big eighter at the front of the group shook a fist at Chet and said something that looked and felt like a threat. But the siren sounded simultaneously.

"Is that right?" Chet replied breezily. "Then why did her father buy a shotgun?"

He would have gone on to tell them exactly why her father bought a shotgun, except that their tightening circle implied that it wasn't their job to listen to bedtime stories because it was Chet McCoy who was about to be put to sleep.

So he dropped the wasted words.

The first man to cross the line had a yen for a bloody nose. He needed one to fill out his personality. His face practically cried for one. If there ever was an eighter, Chet thought, who was born to have a bloody nose . . .

Chet obliged him with a short, efficient jab.

By then the second guard was upon him, so close that Chet didn't have time for another character analysis. In fact, time and space were suddenly so scarce that he could only allow his fist a mere span of its own length before it sank into the man's stomach. It was enough.

Someone grabbed him from behind around the

chest. He tried to break free and couldn't, so he flipped himself backward, landing full weight on his assailant. That put another of the eighters temporarily out of action, but it left Chet at the mercy of the others. As he tried to rise, he saw them coming from all angles. A horde of frustrated guards taking out their revenge on the one and only prisoner left behind. Chet knew he'd lost. But he'd known it all along. Avon had escaped and he'd made good use of a lot of pent-up energy, and he couldn't ask for more than that.

He kicked his feet and mashed a jaw. Then he twisted, grabbing an unmatched pair of ankles and pulling them together with a vicious crack. Two more guards dropped. But the others landed on him as if it were the last play of the game and he had the rollerball. He was smothered under their bulk and could feel more piling on. Arms pinned, legs pinned, stomach squashed, chest squeezed—and feeling strongly jubilant in spite of it—he saw one more golden opportunity. He grabbed for it. Then they were beating his head into the ground, but he hung on tenaciously, and the last thing he remembered was the satisfying taste of somebody's ear . . .

The next thing he tasted swept past his tonsils and left them sizzling. There were times, he found out at that moment, when a swig of Stopper rum was more of a jolt than a tonic, and a lot more effective than a boozer pill. The way the pure stuff went warmly down made him think at first that he was somehow back on *Ruffian* with Rocky, but to his dismay it wasn't Rocky he discovered when he opened his eyes.

830754 stood by with the empty squeezebag.

"Try to sit up," the android said.

"I can't and I don't want to," Chet responded groggily.

"Try."

"Go away. Go recharge your goddamn cells."

"Another drink, perhaps."

"If you want it spit in your face."

"Ah, McCoy . . ."

"Ah, 830754 . . ."

"I must force you to sit up, no matter how you feel."

"Dammit, what for?"

"For Ludinder," said the android. "He wants to talk to you *now*."

The name rambled through Chet's mind like the last touch of the prison siren. He rubbed his head where it hurt most, right under the hairline, and tried to refocus his eyes.

He said, "What do I care what Ludinder wants? I'm not an eighter."

But he was looking past the android, and in three different wall panels he found a picture of himself lying sprawled on the floor. And from around the viewers he followed the bending white beams up to the eighter flag; coming down again he caught a glimpse of the du-metal door that kept suggesting the presence of a vault. He forced all of the gathered sights into a single area of his hazy, hurting head. After a careful sorting of memory it occurred to him that if he turned that hazy, hurting head a small amount to his right, he would see the tiers of colored cushions that led up to the political patriarch of SunStop 8. He didn't bother to test the theory. He knew where he was. He was on an unmerry-go-round. Why was he back here again?

But he was partly wrong. Ludinder was not up on the throne. The dictator was just walking into the room.

"You're feeling better, McCoy?" was his first statement.

"No better, no worse," Chet replied, wishing that at least a few of the pains would subside, or that his head would start to clear . . . or that the android's toe would quit poking into his ribs.

"You must sit up," said 830754. "Ludinder is here to talk to you."

With considerable effort, Chet rose all the way to his elbows before he decided that it wasn't worth it. He remembered a lot of guys jumping on top of him. But he didn't remember being hit in so many places. Gently, slowly, he let himself back down and folded an arm under his head so that he could see what was going on.

He said, "Let Ludinder talk. I can hear him. This floor is cast in my mold right now."

The answer didn't seem to make the android happy. He was about to initiate another kick when his leader, in a benevolent gesture, advised him to stop and came forward. The very old man in his unkempt red jacket gazed down at Chet; and when he spoke, his voice was deliberately patient and barely controlled.

"You're at the final crossroads, McCoy. It's time for the last choice, the ultimate decision. May I presume that you're now willing to direct the lottery?"

"Why should you presume anything?"

"Because of the changes brought about by last night's affair."

Chet frowned.

"The logic escapes me," he said after some thought. "You had my answer yesterday. It hasn't changed. It's even become firmer because Avon's out of the jug."

"Be careful. This is definitely your last chance."

"That'll save repetition every morning. No, pal, I'm not running the lottery."

There was a heavy pause before Pawk Ludinder spoke again.

Then he said, "You're too stubborn to deal with, McCoy. We're finished. I don't want to see you again." Another pause came, during which Chet rearranged his aching muscles and awaited the order to return him to the prison. But Ludinder's words were otherwise directed. "Last night," he said, "you abetted and participated in a raid on government property, brought about by Abraxas. You're now considered to be an active member of the forces of treason. Do you know what that means, McCoy?"

There was a limit to Chet's poise. He sat up suddenly, dropping all traces of yesterday's pain, blowing the fuzz out of his head, staring into Ludinder's dark eyes, feeling lost and helpless and hysterically mad, and still not believing the words that he was going to hear.

"The judgment is automatic," Ludinder said triumphantly. "You will be executed by firing squad on the morning after next."

9.
The Dead Horse Blues

The night after next Chet went to heaven.

If he had actually departed from life and breath, he would have gone full of laser holes in the other direction; but because he was still very much alive, his excursion into paradise was a round (and soft and supple) trip that started with a late evening tap on his bedroom door, thereafter referred to in his thoughts as the girly gates.

Of course at the moment he didn't know he was going to heaven. He had just come back from the land of deep sleep and had barely orientated himself to the idea that someone was knocking at the door.

"All right," he grumbled, and swung out from under the canopy of the satiny bed.

Throwing on a pair of pants, he dragged his bare feet across the lawn of carpeting to the closest point where he could activate the solar panels. As the light came on, he growled at himself in the mirrored wall. From the way he looked, he decided evilly, it would be a simple matter to scare away whoever was on the other side of the door.

But the angel from heaven didn't scare easily.

"Octo, sweetie," was what she said, and planted her finger in the hair on his chest.

He thought about returning the greeting. It would have meant finger contact with breasts that were just big enough to be physically evident under the loose, over-the-head, disposable robe. Naturally he thought twice about it. Then he folded his hands with miraculous control.

"Juell," he remarked, "as was said by the lady with the brand new couch—this is no place for you to come."

She answered by stepping inside and closing the door. "I must talk to you. How are you?"

"Lousy, but it's better than being lashed to the wall," he explained into her brown eyes. "At least they cancelled the watchdogs and gave me free run of the place so I can start on the lottery. But they know I can't get out of this building. I checked it again today. It's tight."

She raised her brows. "But it's my planet."

"What does that mean?"

"You can get out if I help you, sweetie."

"Are you going to help me?"

"Yes," she said. She took a walk around the room and eventually aimed for the bed. And there she sat on the ruffled blanket. "I can really get you out, Chet."

He wandered after her.

He said, "Let's go. I'm ready right now."

Juell pressed her fingers on her headband as if she were reading a crystal ball. "Oh, you can't leave now," she said demurely. "They would probably get another bookie to take your place."

"So what?" Chet asked.

"He might not be as brave and handsome."

"And he might be a lot more of both."

"Phooey. I don't think so. Anyway, whoever he would be, he wouldn't have a girlfriend who is staying securely in the care of Abraxas."

She said it in a way that woke him up completely. As if it were more of her loud hard music. As if it were the headline of a long, long story. He didn't like the way she said it.

"And what makes her a factor?" he demanded, with

the feeling that he'd been prompted into the question.

"Factor?" she wondered.

"Yeah. It means the goddamn price of fish. It means what the hell does Avon have to do with you or me, or with going or staying?"

"Maybe a lot," said Juell. She was calm and serious. "And maybe not so much. It depends on you and the lottery. But don't worry, sweetie. Abraxas has her well hidden and she's doing fine there."

Chet's voice carried stings. "How do *you* know?"

"I've heard," she replied.

He sat with her on the bed and his fingers circled her arm.

"All right, what've you heard?" He was bugged by an offbeat notion that might have been merely the exciting effect of her presence, but he called it a probable eight-to-five that small, sweet, sexy Juell Ludinder was about to throw a jetstream across a Chetstream and give birth to the first rainy day in Decatur. "Go on," he said levelly.

She cleared her throat. "They—the followers of Abraxas—they don't want you to put on a good lottery. They don't want the lottery to be a success." She shrugged. "And they have your lover girl."

Chet pulled Juell closer, but not affectionately. Eight-to-five it had started out. Now it was even money. He placed his bet.

"You're the live-in partner of Abraxas's mind-reading act," he said slowly, analyzing his own statement. "You're the spy. You're . . . Well, what are you? You're one of the rebels."

She nodded. She raised her long lashes.

"Of course I am. Can you imagine me marrying Ludinder for any other reason? I'm too young to be shriveled at." She was one for providing emphasis to her spoken judgments. As her head came down to rest on Chet's shoulder, her slim hand darted back to the hairy spot of his chest; and even after he had grabbed her wrist and released the emphasis, he could still feel the bonfire clear up to his teeth.

He stood up and moved quickly to a spot where he could think. It turned out to be a spot in front of the mirrored wall, as if talking to her reflection would diffuse the impact.

"I don't know what you want," he said. "You're a little bit of everything. You're an easy-living girl sitting on the floor listening to wall tapes. You're Pawk Ludinder's wife. You're a spy for Abraxas. And you're trying to get cozy with me. To tell you the truth, Juell, I don't know how to handle you. So let's talk about Avon. Is she some sort of hostage for Abraxas?"

"Yes, that's right," Juell said.

"What for? To make sure that the lottery doesn't come off?"

"Not exactly, sweetie Chet. The lottery must go on."

"But I thought–"

"And it must fall on its tubes," she explained. "Fail completely. Do you understand? If you go away, another bookie might come and zip up a good lottery. But if you stay, you can ruin the lottery, and show all the eighters that Ludinder is an ass."

Chet laughed. It didn't feel like a happy laugh. It reflected an unbalanced mood that came from trying to determine whether he was being squeezed into a black hole or torn apart by the expanding universe. "Do you know what'll happen to me," he asked Juell in the mirror, "if I purposely louse up your husband's lottery?"

With a quick nod, she raised an imaginary laserod, closed one eye to aim, and pulled the trigger. An imaginary beam hit him in the vulnerable spot that was her target. And it hurt. With her on the firing squad, he thought, a guy would have to let out the hem on his bulletproof vest.

"All right then, honey," he went on. "If I *don't* louse

up the lottery—if it goes well and makes a bundle—what will Abraxas do to Avon?"

Juell drew her finger like a stiletto across her throat.

Chet threw up his hands. "It's like betting on a dead horse!"

"I'm not a dead horse," she replied, and left her seat on the bed to come over to where he was standing. Together they looked into the mirror. She bounced her words back at him. "Don't blame me, Chet. I'm only bringing you the message from Abraxas. From what I think about an Earthman bookie, I'm pretty sure you can find a way to get . . . to get . . ."

"The payoff," he said mechanically.

"That's right, the payoff," she purred, turning to put herself between him and the mirror. Her hot eyes worked on him. Finally he put his hands on her shoulders.

"Juell . . ."

"Would you like to have me now?" she asked.

"Just like that?"

"No, sweetie. With my clothes off."

He took a better look at her. The last time—the first time he'd met her—there had been the blare of all that hard music, the pressure of his sudden kidnapping, too many new surroundings, and his escape from the bedroom and from 830754. Now that he had a clearer head and a more lingering chance to study her features, he found traits of which there had been no prior hints. She looked older now: maybe twenty-eight instead of twenty-two. And with the maturity went a clever knowledge of life, momentarily overshadowed by tenderness and affection . . . Strange things to find in a woman who casually relayed the threats of Ludinder and Abraxas, and whose loyalties were spread all over the wonderplanet. Stranger yet for Chet to discover how much he wanted her. From the corner of an eye he could see their image in the wall mirror, standing close together with the canopied bed in the background, and he could almost see the rest of it wall-projected like an X-tape. Following his imagination, he slipped his hands past her shoulders and drew her tightly into the circle of his arms. His fingers touched the back of her neck.

Juell's tiny, perfect body relaxed against his. When she looked up at him, her eyes were shining; but she slowly closed them and took a lick at her lips.

"I love you, sweetie," she said quietly. "I love you so much."

And that was the night Chet went to heaven. The only way he'd ever get there.

10.
Rules of the Game

Eldin Sanders was a holographer. He was a mild old man who wore a beret to look a negligible five years younger. He smoked brown du-pot through a long white holder that bobbed as he talked, and that movement along with his low easy voice served to relax his subjects and set them into natural poses. In his years in the arts he had contended patiently with everyone from spitting kids to bashful nudes to bearded generals. Recently he had supported Ludinder's revolution by distributing fake holograms of lasered babies and blasted homes to the easily aroused eighters, and in turn had been rewarded when the coup was *fait accompli*. Now he was the official government holographer, and would probably remain in that position until the regime was deposed or until it was discovered that he carried a half-dozen interesting holograms of Juell in his personal portfolio.

All of which hardly describes the aging, raging Eldin Sanders who ripped the capsule from the back of the unit and hurled it into the disposer.

"Goddamn bitch—in—space!"

Chet moved out of the beam's path and took a step away from the background of velveen draperies. "Why did you do that?" he asked blandly.

"Why?" repeated Sanders. "Why? Why?"

"I asked you first," Chet reminded him.

Sanders took off his beret and wiped his forehead. Then he balled up the cap in his fist.

"Ever since this morning," he said, "I've been trying to take a decent picture of you. How many do you think so far?" The du-pot holder jutted straight out of his clenched teeth like an accusing finger. "Ten, do you think? *Sure*. Ten would be nothing. When Ludinder ordered me to make a perfect holograph of you to put on the lottery tickets and in the ads, I thought it would be easy. I took ten shots, and then another ten, and now six more. And they're all no good! How many more . . . Every time I take a picture you do something to ruin it. Look what it says for this one."

Chet looked over at the small screen on the holographing unit. The message he saw was number HL4224X and it read: QUALITY SCAN REJECT: SUBJECT'S EYE HALF-CLOSED.

"Sorry, pal," he said, and in a way he was. The daylong session and the exact timing of physical disorders was not doing him any good either. "It's all my fault. I didn't get much sleep last night. Why don't you pack up your things and we'll start fresh tomorrow morning? Okay?"

The holographer nodded miserably and began to power-down the unit.

Ray Bell was a seller of lottery tickets. It had been his profession since he was big enough to lug around the trademark: a double, gas-paneled, raster screen that hung by straps from his shoulders and covered the entire back and front of him from a point just above his knees to a line across his armpits. Normally this mobile billboard carried a dynamically changeable electronic display of the lottery numbers that he had available for sale, as well as the winning numbers from the previous lottery and a few of his suggested winners to come. One microchip within the screen handled the teleprocessing of data back and forth to the host computer. A second chip controlled the raster reproduction of hard-copy tickets that were given to the purchasers. The third and last chip was a clock type that recorded the hours worked and the kilometers walked.

Of course, all of Ray Bell's screen was blank at the moment. He was among the eighter unemployed. But, blank or not, he was still wearing his electronic uniform on the day he came to Chet's office in the capitol building, and he refused to consider hanging it on the coat rack.

"My territory is the north side of Decatur," he announced.

The words went in and out of Chet's mind like blown-away stardust. He was thinking about Rocky and *Ruffian* and the cool wagerings of Earthmen. "Fine, pal," he replied finally, to whatever it was.

"In my area," Bell continued, "I know every bar that's still open and who's got money and who hasn't."

"Sure, good," Chet said.

Bell tapped his chest screen. "I'm the best lottery man in the business."

"Glad to hear it," Chet said. Smiling amiably, he took the man by the arm and led him out into the corridor where 830754 was waiting. Chet gave the android the score. "This one won't do."

"But he has a great reputation," the android argued.

"Maybe so, but what has he done lately?"

"Lately? There is no lottery lately."

"That's just it. Remember that this guy sold tickets in the last lottery and it never got off the ground. So he's a symbol of failure, a man to distrust, a throwback to the old ways and means . . . Well, we're not going to let him mess us up this time, 830754. We need new blood." Chet hitched onto a passing thought and snapped his fingers to get it going. "Women!" he said. "That's what we need. Get me some eighter girls with high-level breasts, and I'll show you how to sell tickets."

"Ah, but the screens. . . ."

Chet gave it some visual thought.

"It'll work out—we'll just make them into scarfs." Chet's brain was overflowing with dodge after dodge, and he wasn't sure how long he could keep it up; but he stretched out his arm in another moment of drama and gazed past it expectantly. "Can't you see them now, marching down the streets of Decatur, heads high, hair flowing, eyes inviting, mouths puckered, and their full breasts hugged by electronic scarfs . . ."

830754 nodded eagerly. He could see them.

"Ah, yes," he said.

Chet took a grip on the android's arm. "Then go get them, pal, and pick them carefully. Believe me, our winning number for this lottery will be 36-24-36."

And even Chet, who had invented the gimmick merely as another stall, admitted to himself as he closed the door that it was a goddamn good idea.

Todd Octer was a programming consultant. He was tall and very smart and wore his hair in a single braid. It was his job, as decided by Ludinder, to take care of the host computer that ran continuously in the basement of the capitol; and the lottery program was one of thousands of concurrent tasks that depended on that computer. Octer knew them all.

"It's fully debugged," he said. "I've promoted it to the master library."

Chet looked him in the eye. "What is it?"

"It's the new report you wanted me to generate." Octer held up a listing that was evidently a sample. "Remember, you said you'll need a printout twice a day of all the people who buy more than one ticket."

Chet studied the paper superficially. Through years of interaction with *Ruffian's* intelligence, he had become quite familiar with computer data and the art of programming, but he purposely shut it out of his mind when dealing with this man. He just nodded and handed back the printout.

"You know your business," he said. "Now the next thing—"

"The *next* thing?" Octer asked. "You said this was the last, and we'd be ready to run it."

Chet folded his arms.

"It'll be the last when I say so. If we cut this lottery short, Ludinder will cut us shorter." Chet felt a headache coming on, but he put it aside and struggled for some new directions. "We have to solve the problem of the winning numbers. There's nothing more important than the winning numbers; so, Octer, this is what you have to do—I want the computer to generate purely random decimal digits in groups of eight, and I want to be able to control them."

"Random *and* controllable?" Octer's voice was up an octave. "How can a computer do that?"

Chet stared him down mercilessly.

"How should I know?" he said at last. "I'm not a goddamn programmer."

Mak Crosby was bonded. He was huge and husky and took care of a lot of money and never lost a dollar. Nor an argument.

"Of course all my jitters are open cars," he protested. "That's the only kind there are on SunStop 8. It doesn't rain here, and it doesn't get cold."

"But what kind of protection is there in an open jitter?" Chet was wandering around his office, tossing off questions as fast as they occurred to him. "Your people are going to be transporting a lot of money, bringing it in from all the ticket sellers. How do I know that your little jitters won't get knocked off by some tag teams from Abraxas?"

"It'll never happen. We change routes, we drive in convoys . . ."

"Not good enough."

". . . and we have automatic destruction. If anyone

tries to touch the money, he gets blown up along with everything." Crosby pointed at the contract that was waiting to be signed. "I tell you, McCoy, we'll deliver. Every single dollar will end up here in Ludinder's vault."

Chet picked up the pen and put it down again.

"I've got to be sure. How about a demo?"

Crosby reddened. "What do you want to see?"

"Well, the automatic destruction seems to be the top of your line."

"But it'll cost me a jitter . . . OK, McCoy, if that's what you want, that's what you'll get. When should I set it up for?"

Chet counted on his fingers and then closed his hand.

"I'm tied up as far as I can see," he said, businesslike. "How about sometime after the end of next week?"

As Chet walked with 830754 into Ludinder's throne room, he was still plotting new strategies to keep the affair at a stalemate. Now that he was in practice, the schemes came into his head as fast as he needed them—some of them, he admitted, were so practical and so unique that he almost regretted not being able to really try his hand at the lottery game. But instead he spun them into sticky webs that tied up the works and prolonged his only plan. He knew that as long as the lottery didn't get started, he and Avon would stay alive. Once it started, if it ever did, it would be impossible for him to satisfy both Ludinder and Abraxas, and someone on this end or that end would suffer for it. Delay-of-game was the answer for now. With no other recourse, he had to stay on the treadmill and stretch it out.

Ludinder snapped it back with a jolt that hammered Chet's head.

"You're stalling, McCoy," the leader said from on top of the pillows. "An idiot could have begun the lottery by now."

"Well, if you want another idiot's lottery . . ." Chet replied.

"Stop it! You can't talk me into circles like you've done with everyone else. Weeks have passed, and nothing has been accomplished."

"There's a lot of groundwork to it."

"Groundwork?" The old man's face was furious.

"Yeah. Getting things thought out. And getting them set up the right way." Chet leaned forward stubbornly. "Goddammit, it takes time."

"Not this much time."

"Well, I've never run a lottery before."

"I think . . ." Ludinder paused and picked up a pillow. He squeezed it in his hands. "I think . . ." His eyes narrowed. "McCoy," he said, spitting out the words, "you're a liar. I brought you back from prison on your promise to direct the lottery, and instead you've only caused confusion among my staff. I don't need you for that—you might as well be dead."

A hand like du-steel gripped Chet's arm. 830754 was getting ready to carry out orders. Chet saw the anticipation on the android's face and then looked back up to the leader of the eighter world.

"Let me tell you about the lottery."

With one finger Ludinder motioned 830754 out of the way. "Go ahead, McCoy. Tell me what you've been doing."

Chet's mind flew back to re-sort his schemes.

"First of all," he said slowly, "I've got to tell you that my picture on the tickets is a good touch but not enough to give you the payoff you need. I'm sure you know that. If I'm going to make the lottery work, it has to be tailored and attractive and played like a symphony."

Ludinder nodded. Chin buried in the pillow, he waited for more.

Chet began moving around the room to help himself think. "Most lotteries fall fairly flat because they're strictly a luck game. Nothing much the player can do but buy his ticket and wait for a number. That's not much good. The real action in gambling—the fun of it all—is to combine luck with skill. Give the player a little bit of choice, a little something to determine on his own, a little control of his fate . . . And that's what gets him hooked and keeps him coming back for more."

"I don't understand," said Ludinder.

"Well, consider the freefalls. When a guy tries to pick the winner of a freefall, nothing he can do can actually make one faller go faster than another; but at least the bettor can review the past performances, can pick a name that reminds him of an old girlfriend, can analyze the distance between asteroids, can try to outguess the solar wind—in other words, he thinks he's relying on his own brain or his own actions."

"So?"

"Don't you see, pal, it gets him *involved.*"

"What I don't see," said Ludinder, "is how you can do anything like that for a lottery. You're still stalling. You're spouting off in your usual manner. 830754, get rid of him."

Chet jumped out of the android's way and clenched both fists. He knew he had a perfect lottery in his mind; it had been brewing there for weeks. The problem now was to recall it under this pressure and to explain it in the few minutes he was being allowed to use.

"Goddammit, give me a chance! I've got the greatest ideas you've ever heard."

Again Ludinder gestured to temporarily hold off the grabbing hands of 830754. "So far I've heard none of them. It was *my* idea to use your picture. What else have you got, McCoy?"

"Plenty. To start with, solar-sensitive film for tickets. When a bettor strips off the top layer of his lottery ticket, he exposes a phototropic surface that produces a number when it's hit by the sunlight. But the number is *variable*. Why? Because this world has two suns that work in crazy combinations. So the number that comes up depends on how and when the bettor strips the ticket. Pick a time and place. How many suns are in the sky? Where are they? What is their relationship to each other? And how is the guy standing, and at what angle is he holding the ticket? You see, it's all up to the bettor. He wants to try his own systems. He's involved, he's hooked, and he's going to keep buying tickets."

Chet stopped for a breath. From what he could tell, Ludinder was interested. How much he wasn't sure.

"That's the main gimmick, pal," Chet went on, a lot more interested himself. "But that's not all we're going to do."

At that point even the android was showing signs of enthusiasm. He put a heavy hand on his wide forehead, remembering. "The women, McCoy. Tell Ludinder that we are going to use the most beautiful women we can find as ticket sellers."

"You just told him," Chet answered. He stepped closer to the pile of pillows. "And we're going to have plenty of them. In digital scarfs that cling to their bodies. The *only* place to look to find out the winning numbers, and the *only* place to go to get paid off. The purpose of all of that—the sex, the numbers, the money—is to continually bring the customers back to the vendors." Chet smiled at last and spread his hands. "We'll plan to have lots of winners, and we want to have them win out in the open, for everyone to see. Payoffs on the spot. See it in your dreams, pal;

a lottery drawing is going to be a circus event on Sun-Stop 8."

Ludinder was giving it serious thought through his twisted, wrinkled expression. "Anything else?"

"Sure, plenty. I'm still working on it. There's one important thing about it you have to agree to."

"What is it?"

"The prize awards have to be exempt from all other taxes."

"Of course," said Ludinder. In the brief silence that followed, no one among the three in the room seemed to know what to say or do next, and Chet was just about to try to brashly excuse himself and take off when Ludinder spoke again. "McCoy, you are the genius I thought you were." Another silence came and went. "A gambler's mind, a gambler's experience, a gambler's reputation—that's why I needed you here."

Chet relaxed.

"But I still think you're stalling," Ludinder followed up immediately. "The plan is one thing—and it's excellent—but the implementation is another. I'll give you ten more days to put it all in place. Time that you know I can't afford, but I'll give it to you on the strength of your plan. Just ten more days. If by then I don't see lottery tickets being sold throughout Decatur and in every other eighter city . . . then on the eleventh day you'll be executed and I'll bring in someone else to run your game."

Chet's period of relaxation came to an abrupt end. Executed? *Again?* The same inescapable pinch of the situation jammed his mind. His schemes ran out the tubes. His chances, too. He was back on the dead horse, and all he could do was to try to give it a ride. Angrily caught once more between Ludinder and Abraxas, he lifted his head with all the pride he could muster.

"Pal," he said, "you've got yourself a deal. McCoy's SunStop 8 World Lottery is about to begin."

11.
People in the News

For the fifth time in as many sixer mornings, Rocky left his spool room, dropped quickly down the long tube, made his way through the maze of spindles, and appeared at the elongated, computerized desk in the lobby of the Towers. This time he tried pressing a different stud: it was labeled PERSONAL SERVICE. But it called up the same saucy blonde he'd seen every time, the one who for all practical purposes had got the job by listing her measurements on the IQ test. As usual, the screen lit up with a long shot of her full figure and them zoomed in provocatively to a close-up of her gleaming, smiling face; and Rocky, who was frozenly entranced by the opening scenario, watched her smile fade like a shadow coming over the lips of a crater.

"Oh, it's you again," she said, wrestling with a ball of du-gum.

"Yeah, it's me OK," the Rock replied.

"What do you want?"

"I'm still trying to find Chet."

"Well, I'm very busy scheduling the liquid massages . . ."

Rocky put his wide, stubby hand on the edge of the screen as if to hold her there. "Somebody's gotta help me," he persisted. "I've been looking all over this goddamn place—it sure ain't like Wiggen—and I can't find him nowhere. He ain't in the bars, he ain't on the beach, he ain't in the SaunArena, he ain't on the courts or the trails . . . He could be in one of the spindles, but there's so goddamn many of them. I've been looking day 'n night."

She gazed back at him intently. "Who's Wiggen?"

"Wiggen ain't *nobody,*" he said, bringing his face down close. "Wiggen is where I was born—it don't matter, doll. All I wanna know is if you seen Chet McCoy?"

"Oh, that's the fellow you've been asking about every day. I remember—dark hair, tall, gray eyes, you said."

Rocky nodded vigorously. "He been here?"

"No. Uh-uh."

"Maybe he called up?"

"Uh-uh. No."

"Maybe he transmitted some money for the bill, huh?"

"I'll take a look," she said. She split the screen and did a search of the data base, and Rocky could see for himself that the computer's answer was no. The blonde filled out the screen again, shaking her head. "It's still unpaid. We have a collection agency working on it."

"Yeah," Rocky recalled from the episode on *Ruffian.* "So that's *it,* huh? You ain't heard nothing about Chet McCoy?"

"Only what I read on the newstape," she said.

"Well . . . Huh?"

"It was his picture that caught my eye," she explained.

"When?" Rocky pleaded.

"This morning."

"Today! On the newstape today? Please, doll, if you got it, let me see it."

"Sure." She stepped aside and split the screen again, and Rocky was almost too excited to notice that the billow of her blouse was pointing at the scroll area where the news was flashing by, although the breast line automatically etched into his gray matter a notation to look in on her again in better days. "Here it comes," she was saying as the tape slowed to a reading pace. "Coming up from the bottom. See it?"

"Yeah," drawled the Rock. "How about that?"

He looked first at the hologram. Chet looked back at him with a smile that must have been captured in one of his hell-for-leather moods. Probably a starcop photo, Rocky thought. He waited for the headline and the single-column story. Then, brow furrowed, bottom lip under top teeth, he read it, word . . . by . . . word.

EIGHTERS NAME
EARTH BOOKIE
TO ODDS JOB

> Decatur—The government of Pawk Ludinder, plagued by armed and economic turbulence, made a desperate stab at recovery today by appointing Chet McCoy, a 34-year-old Earthman bookie, to direct the SunStop 8 World Lottery.
>
> The news came in a simple statement released through the neutral Titan embassy and gave no reasons for the unusual appointment; however, informed sources on the other SunStops feel that it is a last and supreme effort to restore a floundering treasury. It follows on the heels of the refusal by Bank, Itpl., to grant or guarantee the eighters' request for an internal-affairs loan.
>
> McCoy is a resident of Earth orbit in a modified Class 7 satellite registered as *Ruffian*, and he was last seen vacationing on SunStop 6. He has had rumored connections with a number of infamous escapades . . .

"How about *that?*" Rocky said again, barely glancing at the rest of the newstape, knowing much more about Chet's past than the article went on to relate. "He's on SunStop 8."

The blonde was reading it down to the end.

"Nice," she agreed, very abstractly.

"Like hell it is. Chet wouldn't have done nothing like that without telling me. It smells, don't it?" Without waiting for an opinion, Rocky scanned the selection board and jabbed his thumb at another stud. The blonde was immediately wiped off the screen, but a moment later she blinked back on, gleaming, smiling, at the desk clerk. "Check me out fast," Rocky told her. "I gotta go."

Part Three

CHET McCOY GOES FROM CASTLE TO CAVE . . . AND ROCKY TAKES A POD

3911
SUNSTOP8
Chet McCoy
WORLD LOTTERY
SHIFFMAN 77

12.
Androids Make Lousy Lovers

Concentrated in Decatur—but working all over the small planet as well—hundreds of eighter women were hooked into the lottery network, wearing the newly designed, low-slung display scarfs and selling chances at a volume high enough to justify Ludinder's plan. Although the proceeds from the troubled world were not, and were not expected to be, an all-time record, they were sufficient to please the dictator who was spending a good part of his days watching the deposits come into the vault and choosing from a variety of dynamic reports that kept him up to date on the trivia of lottery statistics.

And from some hidden place in a less-populated area, Abraxas was spreading the word to all of the rebel sympathizers, encouraging them to support and patronize the government lottery. Once a day the young leader would stand on the ridge of a crater, staring at the high-powered scope card in the palm of his hand, enjoying the view of the money-loaded jitters that were passing by on the way to Decatur. Usually he would continue to visualize the loads of loot long after he had returned the card to his pocket and strolled back to the cave.

"The best thing about a double cross," observed Chet, "is that it makes everybody happy for a while."

"How about me?" Juell asked.

"Aren't you happy?"

"Sure, sweetie." She was standing at the mirrored

wall in his room, taking the headband off, letting her dark hair fall to her shoulders. The rest of her was covered by a plain smock, tied at the waist. She was not wearing shoes. "But I'll be happier when we get out of here and rejoin Abraxas. He's a wonderful man, like a god, and there's always excitement all around him. It's been years since I've been with the people I love."

"And it may be more years until I figure this out," Chet said, standing up and closing the programming manual that he'd been trying to read. "In all of these goddamn books, there isn't a single clue as to how to open the vault."

"I know. I've read them before."

"Then we're stuck in this spot and the happy hour's almost over." Chet dropped the manual on top of a knee-high stack of similar volumes and, with bitter feelings, gave the pile a kick that scattered the books over the floor. "You can tell what's coming next—hell and high water. If we can't get at that money . . ."

"Don't worry so much," Juell said. "You were smart enough to get the idea. You'll make it happen."

He frowned. "It takes more than a genius to burgle the national treasury. It takes lots of luck and some outside help. Have you heard anything more from Abraxas?"

She nodded.

"*Well?*" said Chet.

"He's with you all the way."

"Sure he is. Why shouldn't he be? The lottery will collapse, the government will be bankrupt, Ludinder will be ruined personally and will lose the respect of the people—Abraxas's men will be the richest band of guerillas in spacewhere." Chet took another kick at the manuals and one of them tore apart. "But when is he really going to pitch in? And how's Avon?"

Juell handled the second question first.

"The woman is fine. She sends her love. She—"

"*Love?* From Avon?" Chet laughed. "I doubt it. She's probably cursing me from here to the last star of Coverley."

"Anyway, sweetie, she's all right," Juell continued. "And as for Abraxas pitching in . . ." She reached into the pocket of her smock and her hand was closed when she withdrew it. Slowly, teasingly, she turned her hand out and over; then, with the same snakelike pace, she opened it, and Chet could see a trio of pencil-thin cylinders lying across her small palm. "He sent these. Are they something you want?" she asked.

He leaned forward curiously. "Are those blastpins or firecrackers?"

"First quality blastpins. From one of the places where they're tearing down a casino. Like them?"

"Yeah."

"They're all yours, sweetie." She walked over and set them carefully on the dresser. *One, two, three.* Then she turned around to Chet and snapped her fingers. "So there."

"Nice going," he agreed. As far as he could remember, he had never seen real blastpins before. He had read about them, of course, and had seen them used in holoshows and dollar-a-dream sensies, and probably had heard them explode when he happened to be in the vicinity of Earth reconstruction; but there was something nervously different, he admitted, about having them live and loaded within arms' reach, even though he realized they were dormant and safe. To be activated, the cylinders had to be pulled apart at the ends, then pushed back together. In some brief time after that (*fifteen seconds?* he wondered) they did their thing. *But not to worry*—without the pull-push they would stay as quiet as outer space, forever or until he needed them. "Blastpins," he mused out loud, coming over to touch one, but not to pick it up. "These should be enough to open any door. OK—," he came out of his thoughts and back to Juell, "—the sooner the better. The vault is full, and honey, I'm ready."

"You're always ready," she reminded him. "Really, Chet, it's too soon. If we're going to get away from here safely, we've got to wait for Abraxas. He'll let us know when it's time."

"Will you talk to him? Will you tell him I'm ready?"

"First chance I get, sweetie."

"Tomorrow?"

"I don't know. Maybe." She put her arms around his waist and her head on his shoulder. "What's the hurry?"

His fingers formed thoughtful ringlets in her dark straight hair. If there was a time in this whole rotten business when his anger subsided, it was when he was touching her; but even then, there was always a coldly logical brain remembering and recounting, one by one, the processes by which he had come to stand with her. There was no way for him to be content. And waiting was a torment.

"Juell," he said more softly, "it's been a hassle right from the start. I want to be back in Earth orbit, doing what I do. But I had to go across the goddamn galaxy to get away from the starcops; then hounded all over SunStop 6 and snatched away to this place, the worst world I know. I've broken heads. I've broken *jails*. I've organized a lottery. I've even survived a couple of executions . . ."

"So what's your complaint?" she asked as she hugged him tighter.

He smiled slightly. "Who's complaining? That was easy. All *that* was like a sleigh ride on the Mars caps. But think about what's coming, will you? I have to steal the lottery funds out of a du-steel vault under Ludinder's nose. Then I have to escape from this building—which can't be done—and find my way to Abraxas. Right? Somehow, even after that, I've got to get Avon and find a way off this planet. Tell me how I'm going to do all that."

Juell didn't answer. She just rubbed closer.

"Then there's you," Chet went on. "Fooling around with you can get me killed real easily. If your husband even *thinks* . . . Well, never mind. It's probably too late to worry about it."

She lifted her head to his cheek and she whispered in his ear: "Do you want me to go, sweetie?"

"No, of course not," he said. Taking a deep solemn breath, he tried to move his mind to her physical presence; and he found, once he tried, that the mental path was quick and straight and willing. He kissed her for a long time. Then he lifted her, laughed, and carried her to the bed. They were both laughing.

"I can't stop laughing until you do," she said.

"There—I've stopped."

"Not your eyes, sweetie."

He shrugged, to say that nothing could be done about it. The glint was inextinguishable. So, for the next thirty minutes, was he.

There was a light.

Chet sensed it before he saw it. A sharp, wide, angular beam of light that fell on the bed and projected onto the wall behind it. He had the theatrical feeling of being in a holoshow. In another instant, as his mind continued to clear, he had another feeling. Something like stage fright.

There was a shadow.

It grew in the patch of light, like a heavy blanket thrown on the bed. Crossing his shoulders, it went on to cover Juell's startled face, then climbed up the wall until it reached the canopy. Then it stopped and it stayed. A huge, distorted, gray-black mass.

Chet didn't want to turn to see the source of the light or the cause of the shadow. Waking up to both had been enough of a shock. All he wanted to see after that was an open field and an open sky. *Find out more,* he remembered from the SunStop TravelTalk. *Touch 32-0457 on your terminal. It'll give you a good idea of just how much you can enjoy life. And just how much you can live.* But the skies were clamped shut and the room had four solid walls. And a shadow.

At last, with a slow hard twist of his body that took his arm off Juell and faced him to the front of the room, he forced himself, planning vaguely, scheming wildly, to look at what he didn't want to see.

The door to the outside corridor was wide open. The light cast from the solar panels was blazing in on him; that is, the particles of light that could edge around the figure in the doorway; around the massive shoulders and barrel chest and through the open triangle of the big long legs belonging to . . . identity was obvious. And if Chet could have picked any creature in the galaxy to be the invader of his bedroom, his last choice—his *very last* choice—would have been the android called 830754. So, true to some *Racing Form* that had been printed in the cauldrons of Venus, that's who he got. First out of the gate. 830754. A chunk of trouble standing and blocking the only door to the room.

Chet sat up.

The android grunted something that was too quiet to hear, and then added more loudly and pointedly: "Ah, you've made a big mistake, McCoy."

"That's just what I was going to say," Chet told him. "I've been working with Juell all night on the lottery accounts, and just a minute ago we got so tired that we collapsed on the bed."

"But first you took off your clothes."

"Doesn't everybody?" Chet wondered, reaching for his pants that were hanging on the straight-backed chair. By the time he got them on, the room panels were lit, the door was closed, and 830754 had moved to the foot of the bed.

The android's mouth formed into something like an expectant smile; the kind that Chet had seen before on many a man, but never a pseudo-man. "Octo, wife of Ludinder," he said mockingly to Juell. Then his huge right hand gathered up the corner of the blanket and pulled it off the bed.

Juell didn't scream or move. She made no effort to cover herself. She stared back at the giant android, defying him, putting him down, as if he should remember that he was only a constructed servant of the royal family.

"Phooey," she said haughtily. "Monster!"

But 830754 held his smile. "When I tell Ludinder, he will put you both to the wall." The grim humor was all over his face, along with a few other erupting proclamations that Chet could read from experience.

"You're *not* going to tell him, are you, pal?" Chet said.

"What makes you think not?"

"Because you're looking at Juell as if you're naming your price, And because I don't think you just happened to bust in here at the right moment. I think you've been waiting for your chance."

830754 nodded thoughtfully. "I have always needed to try her."

"*Needed?* You're crazy. Androids don't need sex."

The android was not impressed.

"There is no way you can know what I need or do not need," he explained. "What an android, as you call me, needs most, is to be like a man. We are built in man's image and expected to imitate him in a number of limited functions. I want to go beyond those limits. I want to test the circuits. And no one can stop me."

"I'll stop you." Chet advanced a single step and went back to reasoning. "Goddammit, you're an android. You *can't* do it. You could try all night and you couldn't do it. And if you try . . . if you try . . .

You're *ten times* her weight, you goddamn space-eater. You'll tear her in half."

830754 measured Juell with his eyes. Then he closed an enormous fist and waved it in an impatient gesture.

"Ah, I am going to try it right now," he announced. "*You* cannot tell Ludinder. *She* cannot tell Ludinder. He would take both of your lives if he knew you were together."

"Pal, don't make a move . . ."

"Let him, Chet," Juell put in quietly. "There's nothing else we can do. One word to Ludinder from the monster—"

"But you can't handle him," Chet said.

"Maybe I can, sweetie. I can do more than you think."

"No. There's no way I'm going to let him."

The android's smile widened. A flicker of something cruel showed in his eyes, and came again soon afterward.

"If you doubt that I can be a man," he said to Chet, "then I will have you learn by watching. If I can find something to tie you up with . . ." He was glancing around the room, and his neck twisted no further than the direction of the dresser. Chet suddenly remembered without looking that there were three blastpins lying there.

830754 had them in his hand.

Wisely he said, "Ah, so there is more to it than just your bodies. You must be also together in your minds. Is it possible that Ludinder's wife is not loyal even in politics?"

"You're wrong," said Chet, trying to continue the reckless defiance. But within him he knew that there was no use spouting alibis or other desperate lies; for they were caught at it wing to wing like the last bugs of Garth. It was easy to see the future, and hard to accept it. One way or another, 830754 was going to turn them both in as traitors after he finished with Juell, and no words or promises or national lotteries would delay the lasers of the firing squad, or would in any manner convince Ludinder that his wife had been screwed by the android. 830754 had it wrapped up in his gearbox.

Chet took a step backward to the chair.

"Sorry, old pal," he said to the android, as if their sizes were suddenly reversed. "I'm going to have to lock you up in the ultrabath for a few days."

Juell sat up naked. "Chet!"

"Leave me alone," he told her. Lifting the chair to the level of his waist, he pointed its four legs straight at the android. "Get *in* the bath."

830754 thought it was funny.

"I have the blastpins in my hand," he warned.

Juell took the next words out of Chet's mouth. "Go ahead and use them, monster. You'll have a lot more pieces to put together than we will."

Apparently agreeing with that logic, 830754 put the three thin sticks back onto the dresser where he had found them. Then he stretched his thick arms. "Ah, McCoy," he said lazily, suggesting that his life was full of minor annoyances who should know better than to pester him.

"Don't *ah* me," Chet came back strongly. He waved the chair. "I'm telling you for the last time. Get in the bath and you won't get hurt."

The bluff didn't work. The android unstretched his arms and advanced across the room. The amused smile had turned into an ugly expressionless face that could have been the grotesque model for killer robots; and from the way his fists were arranged, he was planning on finishing the matter in a minute or two, and moving on to Juell.

"Mc . . . *Coy*." 830754 came walking.

Chet waited for him, raising the chair up over his

head and holding it there, trying to anticipate the android's first move.

The giant arrived in front of him.

Chet swung the chair at his head.

As 830754's arms went up to block the chair, Chet shifted all his weight onto his right foot, and drop-kicked for the spot where the android's thighs came together. But it was no *man* he was fighting. What might have been a crippling blow against flesh and blood turned out to be, against du-skin and microcircuits, a blow that merely gave him a temporary advantage. Seeing the android's hands drop down to protect the spot from further damage, Chet wound up the chair again.

This time it didn't get blocked. The chair came apart as it smashed into the side of the hard head. 830754 rode with the hit; and although he went down to the floor in a mass of flying splinters, and shook the room when he landed, his eyes were still open and glaring with hate.

Chet fell on top of him.

He entwined both hands into an iron knot and threw it mercilessly into the android's face. He heard the cheekbone crack. He swung back just as hard from the other side and the nose broke off, revealing dark loose ends of breathing hoses.

But 830754 took it with a grunt.

Chet began using each hand separately, sure that each fist he threw at the face had to be the last he'd need, the one that would wipe out the computer brain. But as his arms grew more and more tired, he realized that he was not going to be able to do it, not without a sledgehammer. If anything, 830754 seemed to be coming out of the haze. Chet could feel the resistance starting. The android was rallying with some super rejuvenation, a built-in second wind that was charging through the nerve chips, filling his battered eyes with wild shots of incredible rage. The missing nose gave him the look of an ogre; his mouth was breathing death.

A guttural roar came from the voicebox deep in his throat . . .

Chet felt two massive hands cover his chest. They clamped onto him and stayed there as 830754 lifted Chet and himself off the floor, and stood them both upright. Then one of the hands let go, drew back, and coiled into an iron ball, holding there for a second to gather strength and take aim, and when it was ready it came on like AmDrive. Pinned to his spot, Chet watched it grow. It came at his eyes, his nose, his mouth, his whole face, all at once and fast—a hard, knobby comet—and Chet went flying across the room.

He hit the mirrored wall. From the way it felt, he'd have given any odds that the loud crashing noise belonged to the bones in his back; until an avalanche of broken glass fell with him to the floor, sprinkling on him, pouring around him, each jagged piece reflecting its own jumpy picture of a bed or a bookie or a monster . . . Then he was getting to his knees in the pile of fallen segments, and focusing once again on the tattered android.

830754 came walking.

"Mc . . . Mc . . . *Coy.*"

No human hands in the galaxy could stop him now. Walking: heavily, drunkenly, deadly.

Chet's breath came in short squeezes. *Not quite so damned easy, taking on an android that was built for battle, in a small room in the middle of the night . . .* It turned out that there were no words he could say to himself for reassurance. From this bet on, he had nothing to win. It was, he resolved, a matter of prolonging the inevitable, of fighting to last an extra second, an extra minute—*0234* came into his head automatically and unwanted from the time implant.

He shook his head clear and tried to move. Legs churning in slow motion, glass crunching into powder under his feet, he came away from the wall and circled toward the bed.

Stubbornly, 830754 turned to follow.

Juell scrambled out of the bed and ran to the far corner.

Chet jumped up to take her place. He steadied himself on the mattress, feet spread apart for balance, and reached high over his head to grab the canopy. And with strength he didn't know he had left, he ripped it from its moorings.

830754 lunged for him.

Chet hurled the canopy, falling with it.

From his prone position on the floor, he looked up to see the android's head jutting through the dark blue fabric like a moon in the sky. *Got him!* he thought briefly, and just as soon saw that he didn't. The cloth shredded and came apart as 830754 stood up with tightened muscles. The canopy's framework dropped over his body and hit the floor. The android stepped over it and dove for Chet.

It looked like a falling building. Chet threw one fist upward to meet the face at the spot where the nose was torn away, but it was a waste of his remaining energy. His elbow slammed back into the floor as the hulk crushed and covered him.

He felt a chain around his throat. It was a set of viselike fingers. Pressing . . . digging . . . squeezing. He tried to pull them away, but his strength was disappearing with his breath. He couldn't even close his eyes. *Die with my eyes open,* he thought morbidly. *With my eyes open, goddammit, and my tongue hanging out.* But he refused to stop his useless struggling; hacking at the fingers, pushing to roll over, gasping for a few more measures of air; and all the while there was less and less of everything but pain, and the room began to fade into a swallowing limbo . . .

Suddenly, in the vague image left to his eyes, the monster turned into a *monster.*

830754's cheeks gathered up toward his brows. His jaw dropped. His eyes disappeared. The hole of his nose became a long narrow slit. His whole face twisted as if he were going to sneeze; a horrible, wrinkled mass of du-skin. His mouth opened wider and wider, like a full-blown cavern of Fee, and his thick lips tore apart at the seams. Then it all stopped—except for a few internal bits of static—and 830754 went limp.

Caught underneath him, Chet pulled in deep breaths of air; not knowing anything and not asking questions, just lying in the scraps of his nightmare and weakly prying eight fingers and two thumbs from the flesh of his neck.

He tried to push the android off him, and managed to crawl out from under it. Then he stretched himself faceup and spread-eagled on the floor, breathing more effortlessly, starting to feel the black-and-blue aches, and sorting out the pains in categories of bad to worse. Eventually, as the room opened up to him again in heavenly lights and colors, he saw a naked angel hovering above.

"This, honey . . ." he said to her as best he could. "This . . . this is the way . . . the bookie *crumbles*."

She dropped a cold wet towel on his head.

He held it there and sat up. He looked over at 830754.

The giant android was facedown on the floor. On his back was a protruding peg of white du-cloth wrapped up like a miniature turban. Curious, Chet reached out for it. Instantly he knew the touch and recognized the shape. By now it was a familiar circle that came off nightly in his room . . . Juell's headband!

He found the trailing edge and started to unwind it, glancing up at Juell. She shrugged. "I had to do *something*, sweetie," she said, and looked away. Chet kept unwinding the headband until it came free in his fingers; he stared down at what it had been wrapped around. A weary eye looked back at him. He barely recognized it as his own.

But there it was, his own eye, reflected perfectly in the piece of broken mirror that showed above the android's back, with the rest of it buried deep within the mesh of spinal circuits. 830754 was dead.

13.
Nobody's Vault

"An android is dead," Chet explained conversationally, "when the cost to repair him is more than the cost to construct a new one. And that's figured on the current book value, after depreciation. Then there's the matter of risk. If *one* loose chip is left floating around, if *one* circuit is not perfectly reconnected, if *one* microgamete is overcharged . . . The results are dangerously unpredictable." Tiredly, he had returned to the room and was sitting on the bed watching Juell put herself back into the smock. "The repair technology has lagged far behind the quality control of new builds. Furthermore—"

"I don't know what you're talking about," she said as she popped up through the head seal, frowning.

"By any of those tests," Chet continued, "830754 is dead. His number is retired."

With a twist of the tie, she pulled in the smock at the waist. Her headband, Chet noticed, was still lying on the floor with the broken glass, and she ignored it. "Where did you put the monster?" she asked.

"Well, he's in the ultrabath."

"Is that smart, sweetie?"

"It's as smart as I can get," he said. "He's bound to uncurl the morning maid, but if we chuck him out in the hall or out the window, somebody'll find him even sooner. This way we've at least got the rest of the night." He looked into other pieces of the broken mirror, but nothing bounced back to ease his thoughts.

He had never considered himself a worrier. After a number of years in the business he was in, he had learned that it was usually, in any case, too late to worry. But none of that great philosophy seemed to apply to the situation he was in: where the sudden and unexpected destruction of Ludinder's android had messed up all of his intricate plans and future timetables that might have led to a successful escape—even then, it had been a hundred to one; now it wasn't even ready to be recalculated. He found that talking it over with Juell gave him some degree of external calmness. But there were other factors. His body, especially his throat, was marked and hurting from the fight and not prepared for too much more; and his mind, especially the part that always figured the odds, was acutely aware of the hot and cold fact that 830754's death—or irreparable status—presented him with a challenge that at its best was at its worst.

"To what?" Juell asked after a short wait.

He focused on her again. "Sorry, honey . . ."

"The rest of the night," she echoed. "What are we going to do with the rest of the night?"

"Well, we're not going back to bed. Other than that, I haven't decided."

"If we could get rid of the monster . . ."

"Forget it," Chet said. "Leave him where he is. This isn't a lonely cabin out in some crater; we can't just bury him in the backyard. And look at this *room*. Even if we could find some way to disintegrate the body, he'd still come up missing in the morning, and anybody who looked at this room could put two and two together."

She agreed with an appropriate throaty sound.

"So," he went on, getting up from his seat on the edge of the bed, "we've got the rest of the night to save our goddamn necks."

"*Your* neck, sweetie," she returned.

He raised an eyebrow. He couldn't tell if she was serious, but she was certainly right. Her only known connection with him had been wiped out with the brain cells of the android.

He said, "OK, Juell. You can hustle back to your own room and no one will ever know the difference." He walked toward her, kicking up pieces of glass. "Go ahead."

"No, I wouldn't," she said, shaking her head.

"It's not a bad idea."

"It's a terrible idea. No, Chet."

"Why not?" he persisted sharply. He put his hands on her small shoulders. "Never mind, I think I know. It's because you're one of the rebels—a spy for Abraxas—and you've got your assignment to take care of. Abraxas is waiting for us to bring him the lottery money, and if you leave me alone I'm liable to forget the whole bit and get blasted trying to get out the gates. Then where would you be, honey?" He gave her the answer. "Stuck here with Ludinder and messed up with your boss."

Her eyes got wet, but not wet enough to put out the fire.

"Sure," she said quietly. "That's why I'm staying with you."

"Isn't it?"

"Didn't I just say so?"

"Not like you meant it."

"Phooey. Damn you."

"Look," he said, "I'm not reading you at all."

"You don't have to." She shook out of his grip and turned away. He went after her, turning her back. She was crying. "I can't help it, Chet, any more than you can. You're the same. How many . . . how many things have you done to take care of Avon?"

The name hit him directly in the pit of the stomach.

"Hey! I almost forgot about *her*. Dammit, I can't

just try to bust out of here and head for home. If Abraxas doesn't get his hands on the loot from the lottery . . ."

"You see how it is?" Juell pointed out. "Just like that you change your plans, to much more dangerous plans, because you love her."

"Avon?" It was an incredible thought.

"But I understand. She has red hair and a much fuller body. If I were a man . . ."

He frowned. "I'm not in love with Avon. I hardly know her. She's a sixer. I met her once and never touched her."

"Then what are you so worried about?"

"Well, it was my fault." He remembered her floating in the SaunArena, cautious and frightened, warning him about the eighters; and he remembered her a while later, being dragged into the throne room, screaming and cursing. Then pushed off to Abraxas during the jailbreak. The last he had seen of her. "I got her into this and, goddammit, I'm going to get her out."

Juell rubbed her eyes dry.

"We're wasting time," she said. "There are only a couple of hours of darkness left, and once the sun rises, we will be in the phase of a double-plus day going right into the other sun." She paused. "I wish we could wait. If we don't have help from Abraxas, it could be very difficult."

"If not impossible," he added, but he knew that all the waiting time had been used up when 830754 was deposited in the ultrabath. "Getting the money, getting out of here, getting through to Abraxas—all on our own. But it's either that or the firing squad." He gave it some extra thought. "You know, honey, getting back to what we were talking about, there *really is* no use donating two necks when one will do."

She folded her arms. "Don't be a hero with me, sweetie."

"It just makes more sense."

"It does not. You can't even get to the money without my help. And I'm not going to be left behind with my shriveled husband, no matter what you say."

"All right, I hear you." Chet took her shoulders again, and she stepped up to him, face tilted and eyes shining. He kissed her lightly on the mouth. "Well then," he said with a very faint smile, "let's give it a try."

Chet hoped that the money from the vault would fit into the two suitcases. The bags, somewhat battered from space and time, had carried his clothes—a few favorite permies and many vacationlike disposies—from *Ruffian* to SunStop 6 to SunStop 8; now they were empty except for the three blastpins that were concealed in the smaller one. So with a bag in each hand, he moved cautiously down the wide corridor right behind Juell Ludinder and her wifely authority, which so far and so good had kept them from being challenged by any of the inner patrols, although at times it appeared that the threat was barely suppressed.

But in the vestibule on the other side of the double doors, a tall, thin guard was alert enough to step in their path and put a hand on the blaster he kept at his side.

"Octo," he said suspiciously, even though he appeared to recognize both the wife of Ludinder and the bookie from Earth orbit. Juell took him on first.

"Octo to you, too," she said with a sexy smile. "Can we go in, please?"

The guard stiffened. "No, I don't think so. I'm not supposed to let *anyone* in. The room is closed for the night." He glanced down at the bags in Chet's hands. "I can't let you in, either of you."

"Well, the reason we're here . . ." Jeull began, and trailed off with a desperate look up to Chet. He picked it up as smoothly as he could.

"—is because poor Pawk can't get to sleep," he explained.

Juell nodded. "My husband is having another one of those *terrible* nights. Tossing and turning and moaning."

"I'm sorry to hear that," the guard replied loyally. "But a man of his age with his responsibilities—it's a wonder that he can ever get any peaceful sleep."

"Yes, he has a lot on his mind these days," she said. "What he needs to rest easily is a couple of his pillows. That's why we're here. We've come for the pillows."

"He wants a blue one and a green one," Chet put in, and was relieved to see it register convincingly on the face of the man in uniform.

"Of course," said the guard. "I'll get them for you immediately." He turned and slid open the door to the royal reception room, and went on in, with Chet and Juell right behind him. "When I was young," he went on, "I had a stuffed dog that gave me the same kind of comfort and security as these pillows give to Ludinder. Later on it was my wife. Now I don't have the dog or the wife any more; but, fortunately, I'm here on night duty most of the time. *Blue and green,* you said." He took his right hand off the blaster. He selected two fine cushions from the pile in the middle of the floor, and tucked one under each arm. When he turned around, he found a large suitcase coming rapidly toward his head . . .

Chet examined the dent in the bag.

"It'll hold up for one last trip," he said. "Let's see what we can do about filling it with eighter dollars."

"Well, there's the vault," Juell replied. She was coming back from closing the entrance door; she stopped to open the smaller suitcase, then walked over to Chet and handed him the blastpins. With her other hand she poked him in the stomach. "That's just to wake you up," she said. "Get going, sweetie."

He didn't need the supplemental prodding. If there

was ever in his whole life a job that he wanted to be over and done with, it was this caper from beginning to end. And he didn't know where this moment was on the time line. *The middle? Two-tenths from the end? Where?*

Physically, he knew right where he was. He was standing in the domed room directly under the brilliant eighter flag, with three blastpins in his left hand; and off to his right, between two of the curved beams, was the door to the vault.

He walked up to it. Using his free hand, he ran his fingers along the outer seams, slightly over his head and an additional arm's length out to each side. From that he was able to determine, to his consternation, that the full perimeter of the vault door butted solidly against the wall into which it was embedded, without the slightest ridge to mark its joining. He stepped back, sighed, and ran his tongue over the edge of his teeth. Then he moved forward again to inspect the surface of the door. Meticulously, shifting up and down and across, he studied and felt the texture of the entire slab, arriving at somewhat the same unfortunate conclusion. The surface was perfectly smooth: not a niche, not a handle, not even a factory blemish.

"Hurry," Juell was saying.

He didn't answer. He went to his knees to check the bottom of the door. It was flush the full width, digging deeply into the carpeting. Chet stood again, slowly, eyeing the whole hunk of du-metal that rose in front of him like the thick barrier to the AmDrive engines.

Then he glanced down at his handful of blastpins.

He said, "I could do just as well with wax candles."

"Candles?" Juell asked.

"Yeah."

"Phooey. You can't blow up a vault with wax candles."

"You're so goddamn right."

"I don't know what you mean."

"I can't do it. I can't blow up this vault with candles *or blastpins.* Do you want to know why?"

She shook her head. "Why?"

"Well, it comes to me rather late," he admitted, squeezing his hand around the potent but useless sticks. "But—*I don't know how.*"

"Just . . . just blow it up," she advised.

"It's not that simple. What do I do? Pull the pins and toss them at the door? That might make a lot of noise, but it won't open it." To demonstrate, he ran a hand diagonally across the polished surface of the door, and patted it a couple of times so she could hear the solid clunk of impenetrable du-metal. "Seems to me that you have to have some entry point, or that you have to drill holes in the right places, and a laser won't do it. I don't know the right places and I don't have any kind of drill. In other words, honey, this job takes a pro."

"Can't you try?"

"Sure. And it's odds-on that you and I get torn into little pieces while the door stands fast." He put the three blastpins back into the smaller suitcase and snapped it shut.

He was accustomed to better results. It was no sin, he thought between hard breaths, to be less than an expert at safecracking; the sin was in overlooking his own shortcomings. The blistering night, starting when the android had invaded the bedroom, had caused him to move and plan too fast, too daringly, too recklessly; and as a result they were caught in the middle of their hasty attempts at looting and leaving, with obviously burnt bridges behind them and a smooth thick black wall in front of their faces. *The vault.*

A new idea came into his head.

He wondered if it was any better than those that had come before, or if it was just a tempting kin to the sloppy diagrams he'd chalked up so far. But the more he thought about it, the more he liked it.

And the more he liked it, the more he investigated it. A quick look around at all the electronicaides set into the walls between the beams. A selection of the one closest to the vault. A stroll over to it. A study of its keyboard: a square of nine digital keys, with a zero key at the bottom. A decision.

"Juell," he said at last, "we almost missed a good bet. The reasonable way to open this vault, and the *only way* for us, is to touch in the right sequence of numbers."

"I don't know the numbers, sweetie."

He shrugged. "Somebody does."

"The monster did."

"Who else?"

"No one at all." Juell said it as if she hated to wreck the plan, but that the facts were there, like them or not, and so, still, were the blastpins. "Only Ludinder himself," she concluded.

"He's as good as anyone," Chet said.

"But Pawk—he'd die first."

"Maybe he would if we tried to force him. But he *wants* to open the vault."

Her eyebrows raised a notch. "He wants to?"

"Sure. He can't wait to get it open."

"Phooey." Her hand was on her hip. "Why does he want to so much? You're crazy, Chet. I tell you, he'd die first. I know my husband."

"So do I," Chet told her. He took about ten steps away from the wall and stood there, looking at the middle of the room; then he wheeled, looking back at the vault. He was contemplating the setup and arranging the future as if it were a new and intricate play for the underdog 91-man team of soccolo, with him holding the bets. "If Ludinder thinks that he's been burglarized . . ." he mused aloud, before he ran it on to Juell. "Look, honey, your husband arrives in his nightshirt. He sees the guard lying unconscious in front of the vault, he sees some money strewn around the floor, and he says to himself—"

"There's no money on the floor."

"He doesn't say *that.*"

"No, *I* said that," Juell deciphered. She seemed to be getting interested, if not excited, about the idea. "There is no money on the floor."

Chet grinned. "Well—let's put some there."

She patted the sides of her smock and showed him her empty hands.

"I don't have any money. Do you?"

"No, none of the local stuff. *Shit!*" He grabbed his pockets from sheer frustration, but he already knew every card, Earth dollar, and ITPL check that they contained. And not an eighter cent. *Goddammit, all he needed. was* . . . He snapped his fingers. "The guard!"

It turned out that the guard was not a rich man, but he had a few folded bills and a few coins; not as much stage dressing as Chet would have liked, but enough to calm him down again and start him working hard. He spread the money around the floor. He dragged over the unconscious guard and dropped him in front of the vault. He still wasn't satisfied; it needed another touch or two. Laughing to himself, he pulled one of the heavy chairs to the center of the room and stood up on it; then with a fine leap managed to grab the lower end of the eighter flag and rip it from its moorings in the dome. After he mangled it into a crimson heap, he kicked it over next to the guard and thought: *what else?* It came to him quickly. He borrowed Juell's diamond wedding ring from the third finger of her left hand—one tradition that had never changed through all the spread of colonization—and used it to score a few scratches in the du-metal door.

He came back and put his arm around her, his other arm stretched out to the scene.

"And that, honey," he concluded piously, "is show business."

Juell nodded her approval. "What's next?"

"It's your cue," he told her. He replaced the ring on her finger. "Go get him."

"He won't come," she said.

"Sure he will. But it's up to you to get him primed. Tell him what's happened. Tell him he's been robbed."

"I'll try it," she said hesitantly. She went to the other side of the large room and began pushing buttons at the base of a display tube, but after hitting the second key her finger paused in midair while she looked back over her shoulder, and back again to the tube, before she moved her hand decisively onto the red button that canceled the whole transaction. "I'd better tell him personally," she said, and walked out the door.

Removing the guard's sidearm blaster, Chet wedged it into his own belt. He dragged the unconscious man a little more out of the way. He rearranged the fallen flag. To make the money go farther, he ripped a couple of the eighter bills in half. Then, not completely satisfied but running out of time and ideas, he looked for a place to put himself.

Ludinder's pile of pillows.

It wasn't as easy as hiding in a haystack, Chet told himself, but he wasn't needled. He wormed his way in, artfully replacing the cushions around him until the only open space was a planned embrasure at the level of his eyes.

Through which, after a short and warm wait, he watched the worried entrance of Pawk Ludinder in a nightrobe, followed closely by two armed guards in uniform, and trailed by Juell in the same old smock. She was sneaking puzzled glances around the room, trying to figure out for herself the whereabouts of the man she'd left behind.

Ludinder and his men exchanged a few harsh words. They knelt by the side of the stricken guard and pulled up his eyelids. They examined one of the dollars. They looked down at the flag and up at the place in the dome where it had been. One of the men pointed out the scratches on the vault. A few more heavy curses were added to the air.

Behind the cushions the air was hot and stuffy, but Chet didn't dare make a move. He went on peering through the slit.

In a few minutes—his time implant insisted it was only a few minutes, although in his frantic mental state it seemed more like hours—Ludinder motioned everyone to stand back. He himself took up a stance directly in front of the electronicaide, curving his thin body inward to conceal the keys, and putting his face down close to the numbers. At that point the eight clicks, in uneven rhythm, became the only sounds in the room.

The huge black door swung open.

Ludinder stalked into the vault. His pair of protective companions went after him.

Remaining behind, Juell scanned the area with visible desperation, and was just as visibly relieved when Chet suddenly emerged from the stack of cushions, carrying one of them in his left hand, and a blaster in his right hand.

He gave her a wink for her smile. On his toes, he stepped silently around the flag and the body, and made his way to the vault. He took the cushion he was carrying and set it down in an exact spot at the door opening; then stood straight again and said loudly to all the men inside: "Some nights it doesn't pay to get out of bed."

Of the three faces that turned toward him, two were frantically astounded and one was stone cold.

And Ludinder's words, which came without delay, were equally frozen.

"You'll die for this, McCoy."

Chet brandished the blaster to make sure they were aware of it. "Take off your guns," he said to the two soldiers, and while they were obliging, he listened to the rest of Ludinder's rantings.

"Have you forgotten where you are, McCoy? This is a small world, and it's *mine.* There's no way for you to get to another planet. But, no matter, you can't even get far enough to try . . . this building, the gates . . . impossible. Put down the blaster and beg me for forgiveness."

"I'll put it down your goddamn throat," Chet said.

Ludinder stiffened. "Suit yourself, McCoy. You'll be killed on your way out. My men have their orders."

But Chet was in control of the situation, and the heavy blaster in his hand gave him enough confidence to accept the obvious problems that were coming up next, and which he was determined to handle one at a time.

"Don't make book on it," he answered; then, when the continued afterthoughts told him that the worst could very well happen, that all the threats could come true in short order, he added the words that *might* give Juell an escape hatch. "The thing we do on Earth when we're in a tight spot—we grab a hostage."

"I won't take a single step with you," Ludinder said firmly.

"Who asked for you, pal? I'm taking *her.*"

Juell laid into it immediately with an electric, "No!"

"If you take my wife with you," Ludinder warned, "then your death will not only be certain, but one of slow torture."

"We'll see . . ." said Chet.

"I swear it."

"Swear all you want, pal. Your word isn't much good. Because when it comes to having numbered days, you may not have any more digits than I do. One more shrivel and you'll be gone; if Abraxas doesn't get you first."

"Abraxas is no more than a nuisance. I have him practically crushed."

"That's a great attitude," Chet said, growing more impatient. "You're in for a big surprise someday when Abraxas decides to blow his horn . . . But that's *your* affair. Mine is the money. I brought it in with the lottery; now I'm taking it out. I'd appreciate it all the way back to Earth orbit if you would step out here carefully and get the suitcases, so your boys could start packing." He wiggled the blaster to emphasize the need for quick compliance.

Ludinder curled his lips.

"You should have just done your job, McCoy," he said viciously, and came walking out of the vault.

As he reached the edge of the open door and came around it, he made a sound that was either a grunt or an old man's laugh; at the same time he spun back and threw his small but complete weight onto the vault door, knowing that he could have it closed and locked before Chet could get off a hand or a blast.

He was wrong.

The heavy door swung swiftly to seal the opening. Ludinder's body was pushing to take it right into its frame. But it never got that far. It stopped. It came to within a hand's width of the casing, and it stopped. Ludinder reddened in his supreme effort to complete the maneuver, his knees and hands and chest and face pressed against the du-metal, raging and pushing while the small remaining aperture stayed stubbornly open; and still he went on, his aged body tensed with determination, driving and butting and burning up calories . . . until Chet walked over and plucked him away.

"You're ruining the pillow," Chet said in a fatherly

tone, and set Ludinder down on the floor at a safe distance from the vault.

He went back and pulled the door wide open again. The cushion he had left there was now misshapen and crushed, but it would forestall any further efforts to latch the door. He straightened it out and replaced it. Then he sent Juell behind the big pile of pillows to get the two suitcases, and as she brought them into the vault one at a time, he waved the blaster as menacingly as he could at the guards who were standing there. "Fill 'em up with all the money you can find. And do it faster than I can touch the switch on this gun."

"Don't fool around with it," one of them replied.

"Fast," Chet told him, and used the fingers of his free hand to direct the operation.

Clean clear through. That was the vault. All that remained on the shelves were the papers and documents of government enterprise, and there was no more need for them than there was room in the suitcases. Chet motioned for the bags to be closed.

He was trying not to think too far ahead. He knew that any plans he formulated now, as smart and tricky as they might happen to be, would probably never jibe with the things to come. *What kind of things?* All more or less unknown: myriads of uncrossed bridges and spurs of the moment, building up somewhere in the future to get rid of Chet McCoy, with the same obsession that kept most of the galaxy concocting campaigns to get rid of bookies by any name. It was just a little tougher here. *Tougher, hell, they were out to kill him!* And in spite of the small satisfaction that came with the immediate victory in the vault room . . . *Goddammit—stop thinking!*

The packed luggage was set at his feet and it was time to go.

At Chet's orders, the guards went back into the

vault, dragging the one that was still sleeping. Chet considered putting Ludinder inside, too. If the only man who knew the combination was locked inside . . . He couldn't bring himself to do it. He kicked the cushion into the vault and closed the door.

With the cord from the fallen flag, he trussed Ludinder into an infuriated package and propped him on top of his beloved stack of multicolored cushions. He handed Juell the smaller bag. He picked up the other one himself. He escorted Juell—at blaster point for its effect on Ludinder—to the exit door, where he turned to leave a last message with the wizard of eights.

"Well, I've got the money, pal," he said, "and you've got the time. You might use it to meditate on this problem I have for you—remember, I'm still the director of the SunStop 8 World Lottery, and you can't fire me because there's nothing left in the treasury to pay unemployment compensation. Chew on that, and drop me a wordbeam when you figure it out." But Ludinder was busy chewing on the gag in his mouth, so the barrage of muffled sounds that made up his direct response was more like the far-off ripples of a quasar.

Chet gave him a straight-up finger.

"Out," he said to Juell and pushed her through the door. Side by side, they crossed the short vestibule and went out the double doors into the main part of the building. Chet stopped there to transfer the heavy bag to his other hand.

In front of him the empty corridor seemed as wide and long as the virtual backstretch at the Belmont Studios. Solemnly, he touched shoulders with Juell.

"Which one of us," he said, "was supposed to call the cab?"

14.
The Starting Gate

The goddamn eighters were everywhere.

There were no windows that opened at ground level and even at the most unobtrusive rear door that Juell could think of, a posted guard stepped up to them and gazed down at her for a while without expression, unclipping the blaster to wrap his hand around it.

Presently he looked at Chet.

"You can't go out," he said flatly. "You can't leave the building."

"Then how are these lottery tickets going to get distributed?" Chet asked, hefting the bag. His own blaster had been removed from his belt and concealed in his pocket where he couldn't get to it quickly, and didn't want to.

"Those are lottery tickets?"

"Yeah, do you want to see?"

"I don't care what they are." The guard put two hands on the gun and raised it up to Chet's face. "I have only one kind of instruction concerning you. If you try to leave, I'll shoot."

Chet backed off instinctively and was surprised to see Juell move into his vacated spot. She glared at the guard.

"Do you know who *I* am?" she demanded.

The gun went up over her head so that the blast was still deadly designed for a spot between Chet's eyes. The guard talked to Juell without looking at her.

"Of course I know who you are. Octo to you, Mrs.

Ludinder—for you, anything that you need. But I can't let *him* out."

"Phooey! He's with me."

The guard shook his head.

"Sorry, I can't let him out. Even if he was with your husband, I would worry about it. The orders are very firm."

"I'm changing the orders," she said, moving closer to interfere with his stance. But he stepped around her easily and regained his position, gently shoving her off to one side with the upper part of his arm. At the touch, she started to scream. "Leave me alone, you idiot! Leave me alone!"—and she began fighting wildly, crazily, beating her hands on the guard, bucking and staggering into him as he tried to elude her onslaught and hold his position. "You can't keep me in here!" she was shrieking deliriously. "I'm not . . . bastard . . . I'm not . . . get out of my way!" She was kicking now, and butting her head madly into the guard's chest. "You can't stop me!"

Even if she was acting—and Chet wasn't sure because a lot of things had happened to break her nerve—the shrill trembling intensity of her screams was grim enough to make him reach for the blaster in his pocket.

He barely had time to get it settled in his hand.

Although the guard's aim and attention had been diverted to the urgent need of warding off Juell's insane attack, he had never completely taken his eyes off the prime object; and as he caught sight of the blaster coming out of Chet's pocket, he shoved Juell away with a hard planted shoulder and swung his own gun into the duel.

Chet had no choice. No real choice. There wasn't time to think about it, to think about death or the value of life, to think about what might happen if he didn't shoot, to think about whether the man in front of him had really figured his chances of dying in these circumstances or whether, had he known, he would have opted to disobey orders and save his life by letting the bookie pass. *No choice.* The guard's gun was coming around. *No time.* There was an active, desperate look in the man's eyes. There was only an instant to counter it.

In that bare instant Chet touched the switch.

The red ball of flame burst out of his blaster and blew the guard off his feet. What fell to the floor was a scorched length of unidentifiable mass: a dead black merger of uniform and man. The smell was bad. It was quickly obliterated, however, by the efficient and latent chemicals of the blast itself. And as Chet watched, the body began to crumble.

"Nice going, sweetie," said Juell, behaving calmly again.

Chet didn't look at her.

"Goddammit, it's *not* so nice," he mumbled, mostly to himself. Once before, on a private pod trip down to Earth, he had killed a man head-on, and he hadn't liked it then. He didn't like it now. No matter what the reason. He only wanted to be a bookie and have his fun, and provide some fun for all those guys who wanted to be ardently wrapped up in the space sports . . . How in that simple ambition did it happen that he could kill a man he didn't even know? *What was the guard's name?* Finally he looked into the eyes of the dark-haired girl beside him. *Eighter.* The dead guard's name was *eighter.* Chet was on SunStop 8 where they were all eighters; all eighters out to get him, to stuff him in jail, to stand him in front of a firing squad, to make him . . . *Sonuvabitch.* It was either them . . . or it was him.

His voice picked up a new low intensity.

"C'mon, Juell. Let's get the hell out of here."

She lifted the smaller suitcase, and waited for him to get his. "The back gate," she suggested. "We might have a better chance there. I don't know though. Who can tell?" With that indefinite promise she led him out of the building where for months he had been both a captive and an official member of the shaky government.

It was only the second time he'd been outdoors since the beginning of the lottery.

The first time had been when he'd offered to go out on a field trip to review the workings of the lottery on the streets. Ludinder had been hesitant to let him go, and rightly so, for it was true enough that Chet's real motive was another attempt to search for an escape. Nevertheless, Chet was able to convince the leader that firsthand feedback was vital to the continued success and refinement of the game; so he was let out to roam through Decatur, under close escort of 830754 and four armed guards who never looked away.

"Seems like there's plenty of action," Chet said to the android. "We've run into a vendor on almost every main street, and they've all been getting a stream of buyers."

830754 nodded. "You have done well for us, McCoy. If you had seen the inner city before the lottery began, you would realize that it is not only the money that Ludinder is gaining now, but a new spirit in the people."

"Listen, pal, it's only a lottery."

"But eighters were born to gamble. The eighter colony was created to be the center of legal gambling for all of the SunStops and most of this part of the galaxy. But then the revolutions, the boycotts, the closing of our elegant casinos, the sealing of the parlors, the ending of our games . . . Ah, it has put us to sleep for too long a time."

"Abraxas will wake you up soon enough," said Chet.

"Better the lottery. Better everyone has their minds on the lottery, and off another civil war." 830754 checked their position on the street. "Is it time for a drawing?"

Chet gave some thought to his inner clock. "If we can get to sector 22—are we close to it?"

"Close enough." The android hustled Chet back to the jitter and scrambled him in with the guards. A few minutes later they rounded a corner into a crowd. From the end of the block Chet could see doors sliding open from all of the condos. jitters and sunbikes arriving, and many eighters walking into the area. Some of them, thinking they might be late or wanting a close-up spot, were running. It was, as the android had said, an awakening. An empty, lifeless street turning into a teeming stadium of joy. And a big cheer went up when the sector 22 ticket vendor came into sight.

Even Chet was impressed.

"Wow, who found *her*?"

"We did as you advised," answered the android, getting out of the jitter ahead of Chet. "We searched for the most beautiful women, and put the best of them in the busiest spots. This one, if I remember, is named Nanina and has sold more tickets than anyone else."

"I'm ready to buy a few myself," said Chet.

He didn't know if the girl named Nanina was pleasant or innocent or wild or compatible or anything, but from a purely physical viewpoint he could imagine that half the men in town would be in love with her. And from the way she had slung the electronic lottery scarf across her body, it did more to enhance than to hide the figure that was a winner every time. Short blond hair. A smile for everyone. And selling chances to be rich. *Mmmmm.*

She was probably part of the strange feeling that was coming over Chet, but the rest of it, he thought, was coming from his first immediate look at his lottery in action.

He moved in tighter to the crowd. The guards came with him.

"It's time for winning!" Nanina was announcing with her head raised like a goddess. People all around her were clutching their fans of tickets, some of which had already been stripped in the sunlight of other moments, some of which still carried Chet's hologram, waiting to be exposed to a lucky beam, or pair of beams. He could hear wisecracks and cheerings and a few loving propositions, all in a mood of hope and good times, all with the spurt of adrenaline that comes with the game.

Nanina crossed her arms over her breasts, then dramatically uncrossed them, bringing her smooth hands and long fingers down across her abdomen, where soon afterward, digit by digit as transmitted from the host computer, a series of four winning numbers appeared on the surface of her scarf, flashing in red much brighter than the daylight.

Chet felt a nudge from 830754.

"Watch them all now, McCoy."

"I'm watching," answered Chet, as excited as anyone in the crowd. "Goddammit, I wish I had a ticket."

"I have one," said the android with much less emotion.

Chet laughed. "Well, let's have it. Let's see it."

It came out of 830754's tunic pocket and it was still unexposed. "Where should I stand, McCoy?"

"I can't help you with that. There's no preconceived way. It's between you and the suns."

At first the android held the ticket with Chet's picture facing up and he moved so that both suns were coming over his left shoulder. He looked at Chet for advice and got only a shrug. So he frowned and turned. Now the sunlights were criss-crossing around the back of his neck and meeting on the surface of the ticket. He still didn't seem too sure. He gave Chet another glance, then peered over to see how the basic blonde vendor was situated. He shook his head and pivoted again.

That put the android facing directly into the sun that was lower in the sky, while the sun that was higher was beaming in from his left. It appeared from his expression that he might change around again, but suddenly he made his decision and ripped Chet's face off the film of the ticket.

Chet leaned in to join him in seeing the results.

A slow emergence of the number was purposely built into the exposure, and Chet was pleased to see that even an android could get anxious about it. All the while, 830754 glanced back and forth between the film in his hand and the numbers on Nanina's scarf, until at last it became apparent that there was no match.

"Can't win 'em all," Chet said philosophically.

But others in the crowd were winning. Some, like 830754 had done, were still playing with position; some were kneeling and some were twisting and some were looking for unusual shadow arrangements, and one man that Chet could see was trying to climb up on another man's shoulders. One by one the film-based tickets were turned to numbers, and now and then there was a happy scream.

Nanina started to hand out eighter dollars with the same finesse she had shown from the start. People were waving money, congratulating winners, buying tickets for the next round, continuing to generate a new wave of enthusiasm.

"Chet McCoy!"

He had been spotted from his holograph by someone in the crowd. When he heard the shout of his name, he tried to break away and get back to the jitter, but a whole band of eighter citizens surrounded him before he could take a second step.

"Chet McCoy!"

They were shaking his hand.

They were pounding him on the shoulders.

They were telling him stories.

And a short, very fat man, with thick fingers full of dollars he had just won, was hugging him with both arms and crying into his chest.

"Hold on, McCoy," said 830754, caught unaware by the rush. "We will get you out of here."

"I'm OK, pal," Chet replied.

He was in the midst of his own doing, watching it all happen and marveling at it. He had never thought of himself as an administrator. Or an executive. For in all his years as a bookie he had operated independently, unsyndicated, controlling only the narrow limits of himself and Rocky (and who could really control Rocky?)—until this strange time arrived when he was pushed into masterminding a planetwide organization. He was amazed at the results. It was all working the way he'd dreamed it up: the vast intricate network and convoluted technology, conceived in desperation and bitterness, and plotted under death threats with devious malingering. How had it all emerged? What was it inside him that had taken over? Here it was—he was the champ—receiving the hugs and kisses of grateful winners and the shouts of all the enthusiastic players. A new zest had opened up the sleepy streets of a wonderplanet that had passed its peak—and now was trying to remember again, through *his* lottery, the great supercharged way of life that had been around every day when the economical body and emotional soul of the world had hung on the spins of the microdice.

And as he stood there wrapped in the heavy arms of the eighter who was still crying with joy, he had seriously wondered why he wanted to escape from this power and this fame and this place that adored him . . .

But now, hurrying through the palace grounds with Juell and the bags of money, he had no more choice.

830754 was smashed to death. A guard was burnt to ashes. Ludinder was robbed of a wife and a treasury. It was very clear to Chet that nothing he could do from then on could restore him to that temporary, almost satisfying role of an eighter hero; in fact, considering the circumstances of the last few hours, he could not imagine that anyone on any world anywhere could be more of a hated, hunted fugitive.

"I don't know what we can do," Juell was saying. "These bags—"

"Tell them the same story," Chet said. "But make it a short one."

She considered it. "Phooey."

"That's *too* short."

"No, Chet, I can't think straight."

"Tell them I'm delivering a batch of lottery tickets. That's what we told the other guy."

"He didn't believe it."

"Well, you're the First Lady, convince them. They ought to believe whatever you tell them."

"Maybe, sweetie. But if they want to see—"

"Then I'll blacken their goddamn eyes." Chet returned the blaster to his pocket and straightened his belt. "Keep going." He caught up to her, matching her stride, then setting the pace: not too fast and not too slow, down the long, twisting walk.

The fringe of the day's first sunrise was showing on the horizon while the solarized walls of the building and the panels out on the fences were growing dim with the exhaustion of yesterday's energy capture. At this changeover point, there was just enough light for a gloomy portrayal of the footpaths and jitter roads that wound through the clusters of spread trees and presumably arrived at one of the two exit gates. The huge leaves of the spread trees—blue-green and bananalike—were barely adrift on the soft mellow breeze that was traditional for the SunStops. To Chet, the predawn air was a refreshing experience, and one he needed badly, although it would have had more effect after a full night's sleep. *Had he had any sleep at all?* He couldn't remember. Perhaps there had been some before the android broke into the room . . .

"Can you manage that bag?" he asked Juell. His own was getting heavier by the minute.

"I can carry it a while more," she said in spite of the strain that was beginning to tighten the smooth lines of her face. "You can't take both. You might need a free hand."

"OK, but if you want to rest . . ."

"No rest, sweetie." She examined him for a second or two. "Walk boldly. Be like a man on a government mission."

"Sure," he said, pulling back his shoulders and pressing on toward the gate. "We're going to get out of here, Juell. This is the last goddamn time–"

"*Sh-h-h,*" she told him, frowning. "They'll hear you."

They might have. They were that close.

Both of the guards were tall and wide and formidable. They were standing with laserods in front of the gate. To the best of Chet's knowledge, laserods were not as physically devastating as blasters, but were equally effective at close range and very accurate at a distance. Normally they were worn like swords at the side; however, the guards had them in their hands and angled across ther chests in a ready position.

Chet was not that ready. He glanced at the high fence that ran out from each side of the gate. From what he had heard, the fence was so powerfully charged that it could kill you before it was actually touched. *So much for that.*

He put down the bag and walked up to one of the guards.

"I'm Chet McCoy," he said. "I run the lottery."

That was the last smooth moment in the conversation. From then on the edges got rougher and the voices got higher. The more Chet tried to explain his urgent mission, the more he got rebuked; the more he tried to press his authority, the more he was referred to a higher authority; and the angrier he got, the meaner and more stubborn they got. Not only were the pair of guards of similar stature, they also seemed to be of a single mind. There was no weak one to be worked on. Nevertheless, because the alternatives were not occurring to him, Chet kept on talking, hollering, reasoning, twisting the laws of logic until they resembled the old Einsteinian theories, and all the while aware that somewhere behind him time was running out.

"I'll have you space-chewers up in front of Ludinder himself," he threatened finally; and at that point Juell stepped in front of him and cut him off.

Then Chet stood back idly, only half-listening to her continuation of the effort while his mind pondered the impossibility of doing something else. He had already ruled out going over the fence. *The front gate?* Probably worse, probably more than two guards. Through his thoughts he could sense the highs and lows of Juell's discussion, but he had no feeling for the progress until she came back with a report.

She threw up her hands.

"They won't do it," she said. "You can't get out this way."

Chet's brows knotted. "You told them I had to get these tickets into Decatur?"

"I told them, sweetie."

"Well?"

"Contrary to their orders. They've been told that the Earthman can't leave without the personal approval of Pawk Ludinder."

"You're his wife."

"They *know* that." She sat down despondently on

the large bag. "I'm only his wife, I'm not Ludinder." She looked at the ground at her feet. "It's my fault, Chet."

"Take it easy," he said, hoarse from talking.

The only thing he knew was that he had to do something.

The guards were constantly alert. Their laserods were no longer across their chests. They were pointed, from two separate angles, at Chet, daring him to take the test.

He had to go back, he told himself. *Or he had to go through that gate.*

Either road promised oblivion. In the building he had just left, Ludinder might have already been discovered or might have freed himself, and was gathering all the troops to start the chase . . . While in front of him, the only way out was an impassable archway. Chet looked again. If he attacked either of the tough gatemen, by hand or by blaster, the other would surely be quick on the trigger.

He pondered it briefly.

"Juell," he said at last, "you'd better wander back and try to make amends."

She started to shake her head. "What'll you do, sweetie?"

"I'm going through this gate."

"No, it's impossible!"

He shrugged, believing her.

"There's always the one-in-a-million," he said. "Anyway, it's still *my* choice of how I want to take the shot . . . with a fight . . . or with a blindfold. But, honey, one lamb will do nicely for this slaughter, so if you—" He swallowed the rest of the words, losing breath and voice in a sudden fever that surged through his head.

He stared in shock at the sight, the vision, the incredible dream that had brought it on. And as he stared, it became less of a mirage and more of a miracle.

A thick, muscular, hairy arm was reaching out from the shadows beyond the gate, and it was slowly encircling the neck of the farther guard.

15.
The Rocky Road

Chet said something to himself and didn't hear a word of it. He was too overwhelmed for straight-out thoughts. It was purely by instinct that he dropped the suitcase to the ground and reached inside his pocket for the blaster; all the while watching the poetic movements of the hairy arm.

It couldn't be.

The arm extended through the bars of the gate, stretching and curving and curling, as if it were seeking its meat via Tabtanian antennae. Then, in a quick short sweep, it came around the guard, tightening on his throat and yanking him back hard against the gate. An awful sound came coughing out of the guard's mouth. It would be a time-and-a-half, Chet thought, before that Adam's apple would bob again with anything more coherent. And the arm did not let go.

Dammit, it couldn't be.

The second gateman heard the groan and swung around to look at his companion. It only took an instant for him to adjust; then the laserod was up and ready with a bead on whatever it was that was in the shadows. In another instant he would have squeezed the trigger. Or shouted for help. In another instant he would have done any number of things to free his squashed and breathless buddy whose eyes were popping and whose hands were clawing more and more feebly at the arm that had him pinned . . . But that other instant was not in Chet's plan. And the second guard did not know that the man who was supposed to be on a government mission with Ludinder's wife would smash him on the head the first time his back was turned.

Chet hit him with the butt end of the blaster.

He watched the man drop to make sure he'd put enough muscle into the blow. Then he looked over at the other guard, but no further action was required there. That guard was slowly sinking to the ground; finally sitting with his back to the gate, eyes closed, tongue hanging out, limp and unconscious.

"Abraxas watches over all of us," Juell spouted gratefully.

"Think so?" Chet said. He was looking for something to unlatch the gate and concurrently wondering about the miraculous helping hand. It was gone from his sight but not from his mind. *It couldn't be.* That arm from nowhere. He was bothered by it. He felt that he should know more than he knew. There was something about that arm . . . At last he found the keycard in the guard's pocket and stuck it into the slot in the gate. A whirring sound confirmed the computer connection. As the gate swung away from him, he hurried through the opening, with the suitcases and Juell, walking into the morning's disappearing shadows to see what he could see . . .

"Sonuvabitch," someone was mumbling. "Got a cramp in my leg from so much goddamn sitting around. Shoulda pulled the eighter bastard right through the gate and broke every one of his bones."

Chet didn't need to take another step.

That *voice.* A rasping sound that fit the roughness of the strange-from-spacewhere arm. And between Chet and the first rays of the first sun, a backlighted silhouette of a short and square figure, half bent over, rubbing the calf of a leg . . . It all formed a picture that didn't belong on this world. Surreal. An incredible fantasy, a quirk in a dream; yet existing in spite of the physical, mental, moral, and logical facts that denied it in double trump from here to Earth orbit.

"Rocky!" he said. "God in space! Ho . . . lee . . . god . . . in . . . space!"

"Aw, hi, Chet," was the modest response.

"How did—how *can* you be here?"

"Been here all day and night, too. Them jokers wouldn't let me in. Shoulda broke his neck. Are we on the lam or something?"

"I still can't believe it," Chet said. "This is *SunStop 8*."

Rocky straightened up, testing his leg.

"Well, I dunno how they say it in Decatur."

"Say what?"

"On the lam. Are we or ain't we."

Chet glanced back at the fallen gateman and down at the two bags of Ludinder's loot. There was no doubt of his status.

"We are, Rocky," he said. "We're on the lam. How did you get here?"

"With a pod," explained the Rock. He saw the questions leap into Chet's eyes and he went on hurriedly. "I swiped it. I swiped a soarer, too. It's parked a ways over there." He stuck a thumb in the general direction. "Want to make a run for it?"

"That's *just* what I want to do," Chet replied, and handed him the heavier bag. He picked up the other one himself. Then he took Juell's hand, squeezing it in a way that conveyed messages of love and confidence, of new and crazy hopes.

And they ran for the soarer.

As they ran, a layer of dew squished under their feet, just wet enough to be felt, just loud enough to be heard. From a rising angle the sun's rays blinked in and out of the spread trees, catching gleaming bits of the dew. The day was beginning. The normally perfect day of a SunStop. Perfect. Later on it would be efficiently balanced by the second sun in the system. Perfect all around. For swimming, for hiking, for lightball, for running. Chet ran hard, following Rocky, dragging Juell, thinking to himself between deep and hurting breaths how absolutely perfect the morning weather was, for running.

Rocky skidded to a stop. "Hey!"

Chet pulled up alongside. "What's the matter?" he said automatically, but he could see it very clearly with his own eyes.

A short distance away two soarers were screwing.

That was the way it looked at first glance. Upon further and better analysis, Chet determined that they were only hooked together by du-metal claws. One of the soarers—probably the one Rocky had stolen and brought with him—was on the ground, immobile and unmarked. The other soarer—this one red-emblazoned with eighter military insignia—was hovering directly above the one on the ground, and a hook was extended from each end of its underbelly to the front and back of the grounded soarer. A man dressed in the heavy reusables of a mechanic was walking on the roof of the lower vehicle, apparently checking the attachments.

"They're towing it away!" Juell whispered urgently.

"Yeah," Rocky agreed. "Musta been a no-parking zone, huh?" He turned to Chet. "Good thing it ain't registered in *my* name. I ain't gonna have to pay the ticket . . . Hey, where are you going?"

Chet was already three strides to the good.

"C'mon," he said and didn't look back again. He broke into a run; not as fast as before, more stealthily and less concerned with the weather. The soarer, the getaway soarer, was hooked and fastened and under eighter control. In that condition it could not be expected to fly to the Abraxas crater. On the other hand, Chet reasoned as he pumped his legs, if anyone was looking for three fugitives, they would not expect to find them scooting out on the lam in a government tow soarer, especially one with another soarer dangling below.

He slowed down on the sunny side of the combination. He could hear the man walking across the roof; he could see the man's head. A few steps later he saw the man reaching for the narrow ladder that went straight up to the pilot room of the mother ship.

There was no time to wait for Rocky.

Chet lunged for the side of the soarer, grabbed hold of the window frame and pulled himself to that point. Next, with his feet on the window, he climbed up another level to where his shoulders just reached the roof, and stretched for the stanchion that was on top. As his hands wrapped around the bar, his feet left their perch, and he found himself hanging vulnerably in a useless position. He thought about the blaster in his pants pocket and wondered why people weren't born with three hands.

The only weapon he had to work with was a cheery, friendly smile.

"Say, pal," he drawled with an obvious slur, "give a buddy a hand, will you?"

The pilot or mechanic was a tall thin eighter in coveralls and a blue cap. He seemed at first to be astonished at the sight and sudden appearance of Chet's arms and head, but from his calm second reaction it was obvious that he had dealt with boozers before. "What do you want?" he asked amiably, from the first rung of the ladder.

Chet just laughed and crossed his eyes.

The pilot shrugged. Jumping back onto the roof, he walked over to discuss the situation with his acquired passenger; but by then Chet had his eyes closed and his head resting on one arm, and although the pilot might have dealt with boozers before, he had probably never seen one pass out while hanging on a soarer stanchion. He shrugged again.

Limply, Chet felt the helping hands. They came under his armpits and lifted him to the roof. They came around his chest and turned him over faceup. They checked his pulse and heartbeat. They were then trying to shake some sense and some life into him when he pressed the point of the blaster very firmly into the pilot's stomach . . .

Everyone was talking at once.

Rocky was handling the soarer, occasionally reaching between Juell's legs to throw a switch or turn a dial, and reporting a choppy account, part legend, part truth, of the sins and trails that had brought him to SunStop 8. At the same time Juell was trying to give approximate directions to the remote hangout of Abraxas and the rebels. The police and dispatcher calls, still only concerned with routine matters, were coming over the beamer. Chet had to settle for casual comments.

"I never thought of it making the newstapes," he said. He was sitting on the other side of Juell, talking past her to Rocky.

"Sure, big news," explained the Rock. "Your picture and all kinds of baloney. Well, I can't figger on you going on no caper like this without calling me to go with you. So I figger it stinks. So I'm trying to get here. You know, Chet, there ain't no way to get here. You gotta have papers signed by the space board or something. So whadaya think I done, huh?"

"You told me. You swiped a pod."

"Phooey," Juell put in. "You're drifting too far north. We should be heading out there over the water."

"It's one of those sixer pods," Rocky continued, "that you charter for a space walk with your best girl. So I make like a billionaire and I say to the guy, 'Take me out for the day.' So he gets it all set, you know, all warmed up and primed, and he steps out on the dock to unhook the feeders and—*zoom!*—I'm gone. Which way, doll?"

"To your right," she pointed. "If you can hold it that way, we'll pass right over the city of Matann on a direct line to the crater."

"Hey, that's where it is!" Rocky remembered, and whipped the soarer around to that direction, raising all kinds of mechanical hell with the hooks that were towing the soarer below. And as they came over the water, the load broke loose and drowned beneath them, while their own soarer gained height and speed.

When they stabilized, Chet relaxed his grip on the seat. "That's where *what* is?"

"Huh?"

"What's in Matann?"

"The pod. You know, the pod. Hell, Chet, I don't know Decatur from a clump of starshit. If I ain't lucky, I coulda gone round the world a couple dozen times or something. So I landed at the first city I came to, and it's this . . . this . . ."

"Matann," Juell said.

"Yeah. A goofy, crazy town. You should see it, Chet. They got all these dolls walking around the streets with their tits pushing out these weird scarfs full of numbers or something. Now these ain't bare tits—," the Rock paused to consider how it would have looked if they were, "—but they're really sticking out from these scarfs that are wrapped around their bodies. So I go up to this one nice-looking doll and I give her a couple of superbucks. I gotta ask somebody how to get to Decatur anyway, and I figger I can have a quick lay at the same time. Do I get a lay? Hell, no. Whadaya think I get for my deuce?"

"A lottery ticket with my picture on it," Chet said.

"Yeah," Rocky replied very thoughtfully. "A screwed-up town if I ever seen one."

Chet smiled sympathetically. Rocky's presence meant much more to him than mere physical assistance. The Wiggeneer attitude was contagious. Its effect on Chet was like a pair of rose-colored glasses, a counterpoint to stress and strain, a way to face life on its simplest terms. It was a lift that Chet needed after months with Ludinder. He was glad to have Rocky with him again.

"Quiet," Juell said sternly.

Rocky stiffened. "Sorry, doll. I shoulda watched my language."

"Shut up," Chet told him. "She's trying to hear the beamer."

Chet listened, too. He couldn't concentrate on every word of the messages that were coming in because his mind was involved with too many other hectic thoughts; but he heard his name mentioned a number of times and sensed the forceful beat of the voice. Juell's dark eyes were fixed on the beamer. Her lips were pressed tight together, her hands clasped in her lap. Chet didn't need any more words or clues to know that he was now officially a fugitive from Ludinder's justice. And red meat for the nearest firing squad.

Juell clicked off and sat back.

"They found Pawk," she said, summarizing. "The monster, too. And the men at the gate, and this pilot. They think that you've abducted me and are trying to escape back to Earth."

"You bet your boots," said Rocky. "We'll be in—er—Matann in no time. Grab that pod and be outa here, offa here, before they can even—"

"We're not stopping in Matann," Chet informed him.

"That's where the pod is," the Rock argued.

"I don't care where the pod is." Chet stared ahead out the window at the approaching land, hoping that they had enough lead time to make it. "And I don't care if a dozen Ludinder's are out after my balls. We're going to the crater."

"Huh?"

"The *crater*, Rocky."

"What the hell are we gonna do in a goddamn crater?"

Chet tilted his head a few scant degrees. What *was* he going to do in the crater? The soarer was passing over Matann, and in the distance Chet could see the mountainous folds that formed the wide round ridge of the bowl; from that viewpoint, a bottomless sea of land, a haunted house, an open barrel of a laser cannon . . . And no man in his right mind could have headed for that crater, in the dead of night or on a bright SunStop morning, and not felt that he was leaving the rest of the world, the rest of the galaxy, behind, forever. *What was he going to do in the crater?* He didn't know.

He said, "There's a woman there . . . waiting for me."

16.
Room Service

There was no way to use solar panels inside the cave, so what little light there was came from long-lasting, low-emitting power cells; with the result that many of the paths were in almost complete darkness while others held the eerie effect of torchlight.

To avoid getting lost, Chet followed closely on the heels of one of Abraxas's swarthy lieutenants. Behind him the Rock was stubbing his toes on other rocks and constantly grumbling about all of the environments and facilities he had encountered since his arrival by hot pod on SunStop 8.

"Goddammit, Chet, I ain't even had a chance to get rid of the cramp in my leg, and here I am hiking through the side of a crater already. And besides, I don't like this place. It's all buried inside. And them jokers ain't very friendly and they ain't got no women."

Chet turned his head halfway.

"Well, they've got a *few* women."

"You're kidding! Did you see them?"

"Never mind," Chet said in a loud whisper. "Just pay attention to where we're going. We may have to find our own way out of here."

"OK, but goddammit–" Rocky collided with a protrusion from the jagged wall. "God*dam*mit!"

Chet moved along cautiously.

He was bothered by more than the physical dangers of the unfinished and dimly-lit corridor, and its claustrophobic dimensions. He wasn't sure what it was. Only that deep down it gave him the urge to run; not forward over the steady pace of the lieutenant's clicking boots, but back, away, to hell and gone. The deeper they went, the more he wanted to get out. It had been that way since they landed.

In the soarer, with Juell's guidance, they had had no difficulty in finding their way to the mammoth crater which from the air, even at low level, seemed deserted. They had landed on a flat spot and waited. Eventually, forty SunStop 8 minutes by Chet's implant, a jitter had come for them, and the driver and his armed companion had driven them silently to a ledge on the slope of the crater. A slow and bumpy ride. The unusual canopy of camouflage on top of the jitter obviously robbed it of much of its sun drive.

Once on the ledge it was possible to see the triangular mouth of the cave, from which a number of insurgents had come running as the jitter stopped. All of them seemed brusque and sullen. For people who should have been friends of McCoy, they had seemed more like the Hatfields.

"With all the loot I'm bringing in," Chet had remarked to his cohorts, "I ought to get at least a ten-gun salute. But so far I'm still waiting for the first smile or handshake."

He stepped out of the jitter and gave Juell a hand. Rocky came tumbling after.

"What a hideout," the Rock said admiringly. "When you head for the hills on Earth, you got no place to go but the Hillside Motel."

"I'd prefer it," Chet told him. Something about the crater scene had instantly ground a keen edge on his nerves.

"Me too, Chet. There ain't no women here."

"It doesn't matter. We're not staying long enough to—"

"*Sure*, you can say that. Look what you've been getting."

Rocky's thumb was yanked in Juell's direction, and Chet had to agree that he hadn't been lacking lately when it came to his loving shares. But the situation here was too ominous, too disagreeable to the trigger in his mind, too different from what he had imagined when he planned the escape from Ludinder . . . Chet's thoughts stopped abruptly. Some guy in ragged shirtsleeves was taking off at top walking speed with the two suitcases full of lottery dollars!

"Hold it!" Chet shouted, but the guy played deaf and kept going toward the cave. Chet started after him.

Juell came on to block his way.

"It's OK, sweetie," she said. She had been engaged in a lengthy and serious conversation with a dark-complected man who had come out of the cave. A man who wore a jeweled laserod swordlike from his belt, partly covered by the dirty jacket of what once had been an eighter uniform, now with the insignia torn off, and worn-out black boots that seemed to be too large for him; wearing such things made him the best-dressed rebel in sight. "The money is being taken to Abraxas," Juell explained to Chet.

He looked at the man she'd been talking to. "Is that him? Abraxas?"

She shook her head. "*Him*?" She laughed. "Phooey, he is only a nothing lieutenant. He was sent out to meet us, especially me. Abraxas is waiting for me inside."

"Well, let's go smoke a peace pipe," Chet offered.

"No, sweetie."

"I just want to make sure I get a share of that money."

"No, not *now*. Abraxas wants to see me alone first."

Chet's brows slanted skeptically. "Look, honey, it

was me who brought the bacon, remember? If you think I'm going to stand out here like a damn idiot while you and your leader—"

"Don't you want to see Avon?"

He thought about it. "Yeah," he drawled. "Of course."

"Hey, who's Avon," Rocky put in, but Chet ignored him.

"Yeah, I want to see her," he said.

Juell nodded. "That lieutenant—he'll take you there now."

"OK," Chet said. Although he had been very much concerned when he saw the bags of boodle vanish into the cave, it suddenly seemed unimportant. Avon—the supple redhead he hadn't seen since the jailbreak—was who and what he'd come for. "It's a deal," he went on. "Tell the nothing lieutenant to lead the way."

"Good. I'll see you in a little bit," Juell said, and blew him a kiss with one finger. Then, after a word or two with her officer friend, she walked away into the cave.

And a minute later Chet, with Rocky right behind him, followed the lieutenant into the same darkness. But not down the same path. Once inside, there were plenty of alternatives, crossroads within crossroads. The one they took was off to the left, narrow and dark, damp and musty . . .

Chet moved along cautiously.

The detailed memories of his arrival at the crater were no salve to his suspicions. In fact, if anything, they added worries to his troubled mind. But he knew in spite of those memories that he was committed to trail the plodding boots in front of him, in a slow trek through the weird formations of dirt and stone caused by the chance hit of a meteor some millions of years ago.

"Hey, who *is* Avon?" Rocky decided to ask again.

"Save it," Chet said. "I think we've arrived."

He tried to see past the lieutenant.

The man had stopped in front of a natural archway, and stood back, motioning Chet and Rocky into a better-lighted area. Chet stopped, too, listening—to nothing—then moved on, squeezing by the lieutenant, stepping down into a large room . . . and stopped again, suddenly too stunned, despite his premonitions, to say a single word.

The open area had no describable shape or form, but it was probably about as large as the interior of *Ruffian.* The walls were rough and jagged, meeting at oblique angles. The floor rose from where Chet was standing. It dipped again at the far side. Walls and floors, the pattern was random; no one had made any effort to change the natural design of the cavern, no more than to give it a sampling of light from the power cells, light that put a faint glaze on the rocks that were everywhere, and a blue glint to all the reflections. Somewhere there were drops of water beating unrhythmically . . . Stalactites hung precariously from the top of the cave. Stalagmites were built up in centuries from the floor. In one spot near the center, the two formations met to form a stone pillar, and that gleaming blue pillar became the grim draw of Chet's full attention, and was the reason he was too stunned to say a word.

Rocky said it for him. "What happened to *her?*"

Chet shook his head. It was full of black thoughts. Beyond that and to capacity, it was full of the sight of Avon . . . her chic clothes torn into hanging shreds, her red hair tangled and knotted, her long arms scratched, her hands raw, the creamy skin of her face covered with mud and dirt, and her eyes . . . eyes that were as bloodthirsty as a caged wildcat. But the worst of it was on her left leg. A du-metal chain about half her own length. She was chained by a leg iron to the stalagmite . . . Chet couldn't make his mind absorb it. Chained to a pillar. *Chained.*

His eyes caught fire.

"Avon, for God's sake!" he said between his teeth, and whirled onto the lieutenant.

But the lieutenant was ready for him. The laserod was pointing from one hand. A blaster was aiming from the other. Chet stood facing him, shivering in uncontrollable anger and frustration, digging his fingers into his legs to expend the vicious energy that was held in abeyance by the lieutenant's armament.

"You'd better kill me, pal," he muttered. "Cause when I get a chance, you're first on *my* list."

The lieutenant remained passive.

"Move over against the pillar," he ordered. "Both of you."

Chet glanced over at Rocky, but there were no messages to convey. They were caught. Caught, not by Ludinder, but by Abraxas: by the rebels of SunStop 8, by the liberation group, by the happy freedom lovers, and by—it was an ugly thought but not one that could be prevented—by Juell.

And coming through the archway as if someone had whistled for them were more of the renegades. Six . . . seven . . . ten . . . it didn't matter how many. It didn't matter if they were men or women. It didn't matter *who* they were fighting for or against, or *what* they were fighting for or against. It was what they carried with them that chilled Chet's heart. It was in their hands. It was dragging on the rocks. It was the worst thing a man could see when he's trapped without recourse deep in a cave on the side of a crater beyond the civilized areas of a friendless planet on a day of perfect, perfect weather.

Chains.

Chet backed away.

"Where's Abraxas?" he asked all of them, and his voice cannonaded off the rough walls to ask it again.

The rebels looked at each other. They shook their heads. They kept coming with the chains swinging.

Firmly, Chet planted his feet. "Goddammit, I want to see Abraxas!"

They must have understood the name. It made them pause again for a brief moment, but they also understood their orders. They shook their heads and began moving in, this time more aggressively—until Rocky tamed the whole procession by stepping up to the man in front and grabbing him by the shirt.

"Listen, buddy," growled the Rock. His face was contorted and he was glaring up into the astounded eyes of the man he had plucked. "Chet wants this Abraxas joker and he ain't kidding. Now cough him up before I get mad enough to break your starshit bones." As usual, Rocky knew little about the plot of intricate things, but he always knew his job; and if Abraxas was needed for any reason, Abraxas was going to be had. "You ain't hearing me good," he went on when nothing happened. "I told you we want a guy named Abraxas. Now I told you twice and I ain't telling you again."

"It won't work," Chet remarked watchfully.

Rocky knotted his free hand. "I'll give him a shot. That'll work."

"Go ahead," Chet said. And the way he said it was express permission for the Rock to hit away. At the same time, Chet shifted his weight evenly to the balls of his feet, mentally picking out a bearded chin in the second row of the advancing group.

Rocky hit his man.

The raw power of the blow would have rung the bell on any midway. The man barreled back into the rest of the chain gang, staggered right through them and fell into the arms of the idle lieutenant; and everyone in the dark, damp bowels of the crater cave was moving or falling or yelling.

Rocky wheeled toward another one.

Chet drove past him into the mass, finding the beard he had aimed for and grabbing it with a strong right hand, bowling over two other rebels by his momentum alone. He tried to get to the lieutenant. Guys kept popping up in front of him. He hit them with his hands and knees and his feet, and still there were more. The lieutenant remained at the rear, brandishing the laserod, shouting to the men; and Chet fought on toward him while Rocky pulled men off his back. Finally Chet saw an opening and dove for it, trying to get through it to tackle the officer. But the opening closed unceremoniously while he was in midair.

He collided with a couple of rebels instead and it took the wind out of him. Once he touched ground, he knew he was finished. They piled on him endlessly. He couldn't move. He saw Rocky's wild face in the stack of faces above him—and then it was gone. He closed his eyes to the rain of blows that was pouring down on his own face.

And all that was left were the tons of flesh on top of him, and the clank of chains in his ear, and the cold touch of du-metal on his ankle.

Part Four

CHET McCOY
GOES UP IN ARMS . . .
AND ROCKY RIDES AGAIN

17.
Hanging Out

"I'm well enough to sit up," Avon said.

Helping her, Chet put one hand under her elbow and another around her back, as much in comfort as support. When she was sitting, he let go, and leaned his shoulder against the cool pillar of rock in the middle of the cave. The pale blue light was all around him.

"What happened to you?" he asked.

"Happened?" she repeated huskily. "Well, back in the SaunArena on SunStop 6, I had a short conversation with a stranger who claimed he was a bookie from Earth orbit. That's what the hell happened to me. I talked to you for a few minutes and ended up as the number-one girl in the interplanetary white slave market. How do you like *that?*"

Chet felt his face grow flat and frozen. He looked again at what was left of Avon's clothing. Then he met her eyes. "If they touched you . . ."

"If they touched me!" She laughed with her green eyes welling with tears. "If they *touched* me, Chet? See the black-and-blue marks on my arms?" She showed him both arms. "That's where they held me when they put on the chain. See my hands?" She turned them over and spread the fingers. "That's from trying to break the chain. And do you see the strips of rags I'm wearing? Do you see me naked underneath? Do you see the fingermarks on my neck and the scratches on my belly and the blood on my breasts?

Do you see a woman or a beat-up broad? *That's* from rape, Chet. That's from a guy who likes his daily bit of gory rape."

"Abraxas?"

She folded her arms and shivered.

"Uh-uh," she said. "It's the guy who brought you in—the one with the uniform jacket."

"The nothing lieutenant," Chet said, mostly to himself.

"Yes, him. See the cut on my foot? That's where I kicked him in the teeth."

Chet grew more somber. "I've already promised to kill him, honey. Somehow I'm getting out of this goddamn mess and I'm going to kill him, first thing, in a special way."

"Let me do it," Rocky offered from the other side of the pillar.

"That *might* be the special way," Chet agreed, knowing of the Rock's unique imagination; and he took hold of Avon's hands. "You'll be all right, honey."

She was silent and sad for a long while, just looking at him. Outwardly she had been showing a strength that few women, or men, could have matched under the circumstances. But he could see that it wasn't going to last. She was straining in the last stages of self-control and her moist eyes were turning weary, a glaze of surrender. She struggled closer to him. Forcing herself to sit up straight, she put one hand on his shoulder and looked up at him blankly, almost apologetically, before she collapsed in his arms like a sack of Jovian gel.

"Chet . . . I didn't know if you were ever . . . ever . . . I've been lying here hating you more than I've hated anyone . . . more than *any* of the eighters. You . . . rotten . . . space-chewer. Where the hell have you *been*?" She buried her face in his chest and cried hard.

"Yeah," he said thoughtfully. He looked down at her

red hair. It was long and uncombed. He worked his fingers into the thick strands, trying to smooth them out as a start to reversing the whole eighter process that had wrecked them all.

He was sure no knight in shining armor. He was anything but. There was no rescue inherent in his arrival at the crater, and there was no ransom counted in the bags of money he had brought with him from the neatly trimmed vault in Decatur; and of his entourage, one of them, Juell, had turned out to be a triple traitor, going off to gloat and break bread with Abraxas; and the other one, Rocky, had followed blindly and fought with all of his Wiggeneer ferocity, only to go down in the end and succumb to a set of chains. Chet had walked them into a trap. There they were, the three of them, anchored to a post in a violently formed hole on SunStop 8; and for all Chet knew, some skinny space archeologist in the next century would flounder into the cave and discover three decomposed skeletons in leg irons. And they'd all look the same. Avon's soft tender curves flattened and gone, Rocky's bulging muscles brittle and cracked. *And Chet McCoy.* A big bet lost, the gray eyes fallen out and turned into dust.

But not yet, he told himself.

He was still alive and so was Rocky. One way or another . . .

He didn't know how.

All at once Chet realized to his dismay that he didn't know *anything*. He didn't even know what was going on.

Gently, he took Avon's shoulders and moved her away from his chest so that he could talk to her. He brushed the hair out of her eyes. He kissed her lightly on the lips. She smiled weakly. He smiled back.

"Honey," he asked quietly, "what do you know about this? I can't figure out what I've done wrong. I thought I was all set. All along I've been sort of an ally to Abraxas, and I've just delivered the whole Ludinder treasury to him. So for that, I'm shackled in this goddamned cavern."

He found her touching his hand.

"It's my fault," she said.

"That's ridiculous. How could it be your fault? I mean, you haven't been involved in anything that's happened."

Rocky had an idea. "Maybe she wouldn't put out for him."

Chet frowned. "Will *you* see what you can do about cracking a few links."

"Oh, you want me to bust the chains?"

"Yeah."

The Rock sniffed. "Sure, Chet."

Chet turned back to Avon. She seemed to be recovering her composure, but she was still a bundle of bruises and rags. The sight reminded him of what she'd been through and gave him clues as to what they all were in for. He regarded her uneasily.

"You were going to explain."

"About Abraxas?" she said, and gave it some thought. "Well, he's *un*believable. Taller than you, Chet, and wears a tailored green du-suit that's always immaculate. And the chin, the eyes . . . He's so *un*believably potent and full of charisma . . ." She paused again. "He was well picked for the job."

Chet hadn't been thinking in that direction.

"Picked?" he asked abruptly. "Picked by whom?"

"That's what I did wrong," she replied. As she confessed, her tears dried up and her voice became calm. "That's why it's my fault that we're prisoners. Hell, I guessed it. His big secret."

She stopped as if she were reliving it in her mind. Impatiently, Chet shook her arm.

"C'mon, what is it?"

"Well, he's thoroughly trained," she went on. "Talks and moves like an eighter—even has his hair cut that way. Good enough to convince the natives. But he's so tall, Chet, and that green du-suit didn't come from any eighter shop . . . Mainly, I think, it was the power in his eyes and his voice. Hell, if I was an eighter, I'd be in his ranks myself. Anyway, he was talking to me when I first got here—my head swims when I listen to him—and I came out with a *wild* guess, like part of the conversation, and I hit it right on the button. How was I to know? It was just a guess. A joke. I couldn't know—*nobody* knows—what a Sty really looks like. He was just a hell of a fit for the rumors."

"A Sty! A goddamn Styman!" Chet felt as if he'd just been dragged through moondust.

"Believe it," she said.

"And I helped finance the operation," Chet moaned. "It's all a bitch-in-space! How can you win on this planet? There's either a tyrant or a rabble-rouser or a neurotic ass—or a Sty!—they come and go in one revolution after another. Bounce one off, put one on. Tell me, what difference does it make which louse is up there?"

"It makes a difference if he's from the Sty System," Avon said. "That's why Abraxas can't let us go. If the word gets out that he's been planted here . . . Hell, you can imagine the panic in the rest of the galaxy. And the whole space fleet will be here to get him before he can establish a foothold. The way it is now, it's just another eighter rebellion to be ignored."

Wearily, Chet rubbed the back of his neck. Through all of his life he had heard unconfirmed tales of the only untraceable humanoids in the universe; tales that seemed to have originated, long before his time, out of unreliable reports of things called flying saucers. In recent years the beamer scopes had added some portion of frightening credibility to the probable existence of Stys, but still no proof. The bets were hedged. The Sty System, if there was one, was beyond the reach of AmDrive.

All of the existing star colonies were known to be derived from the people of Earth. If the Stys started there, it was long before the modern era of space travel; or perhaps the Stymen and Earthmen were brothers from another source altogether. Conjecture, thought Chet. No more real than the Stys themselves; no more substantial than the general interpretation that the Stys were warlike and waiting for their chance to take over . . . On that note Chet's stack of Sty matter was depleted, but his mind raced on to emptier subjects.

Like a bucket of his chances.

"If you're right . . ." He told Avon. "Damn, it's hard to figure, but if you're right . . ."

"You should have seen him explode when I called him a Sty," she said.

"OK, maybe he is. Then he can't let us go because he can't risk being exposed. On the other hand, honey, I don't think he means to let us stay here and rot."

"They've been bringing me food all along," she added to the reasoning. She stretched her legs and sighed. "Chet, what are they going to do with us?"

He had been considering it. Or reconsidering it. The new facts led to a lot of speculation.

He said, "Hostages, maybe. For a while, anyway. Just in case he needs some foreign hostages—a couple from Earth orbit, and a sixer. Or later, when and if he comes to power, he might call us spies and let a public hanging be an example to the other SunStops, before he goes out to get them, too. It's hard to tell what he has in mind—he's probably not sure himself at this point—but it's still a good bet that he'll stroll in here one night on an impulse and with a blaster. And blow our heads off. So the way it is, Avon, we can expect to be either valuable merchandise or prisoners or corpses for a long time to come, unless we . . ."

Rocky had an answer.

"Unless we get twenty mules and a laser saw," he

said. There was as much sweat on his hands as there was on his square and sullen face. "I can't do nothing with this rotten chain. Gotta get the key card, that's all. You ain't got the key card, you ain't going no place."

Chet turned his head slowly from Avon to Rocky. He had taken everything out of his mind but the hunt for a next move.

"Well, the lieutenant did the locking," he mused. "So the lieutenant has a key card."

"Hey, we can pay him off, huh?" said the Rock.

"How much money do you have?"

"Nothing. They took it all and left me a crummy lottery ticket." Rocky's despondency lasted only another moment or two; then with a kindling that came from a telepathic spark he broke into a bright, eager grin. "We *bash* him, don't we!"

With a nod of agreement, Chet turned back to Avon and looked her over from head to foot.

"Honey . . . Does the lieutenant still like what you've got to give?"

She shrugged. "Like it or not, he takes it regularly. Every night when he brings the food—he takes me for an appetizer."

"What time does he come?"

"About thirty seconds after he starts."

"You know that's not what I mean."

"So on his next trip, I'll ask him what time it is."

"Cut it out," Chet said seriously. "This has to be done right, and we have to know when he's on his way. Will we be able to hear him?"

"Sure," she replied. "I've heard those boots of his echo through the whole cave."

"Good. Then what we'll do—"

She interrupted with a raised hand.

"It won't work, Chet. He may want his nightly ration, but he's not going to jump me where you two can jump him."

"I thought of that, honey," Chet said. He was studying the blue-lighted surroundings extra carefully. "If the lieutenant wants you, he can always take you off in a corner out of our reach. Or if he's bashful, he can just deliver the food and scram. We can't depend on his whims. We've *got to* get our hands on him . . . and the only way to do that is to get him off guard. We've got to jumble his head to the point of blindness."

"He's not the type."

Chet smiled. "If he's a man, he's the type. You want to make a man lose his goddamn marbles? You want to make him ignore all side issues, including his own survival? And make him forget the past and the future? And see him boil and fume, completely disorganized, completely insane?"

"Yes," she said simply.

Chet held out his hands in a gesture of ultimate explanation.

"Well, it's easy to do, Avon. If you've lived a full life of loving, you've probably seen it before."

She lifted a quizzical eyebrow. She looked at Chet as if she was reading her own past in the anxious lines of his face; then, slowly, realization sparked a light in her green eyes, and she bit her lip in acknowledgment. "Yes, I've seen it," she said very quietly.

Chet was having second thoughts. "Honey . . ."

"No, don't try to talk about it." She covered his mouth with the fingers of her right hand. "I don't need your reassurances or even your apologies. But it *is* a hell of a place. . . . I'm not sure I even know you yet . . . And here in a cave, with chains, with spectators, in a part of your crazy plan . . . Believe me, it's never been one of my fantasies—*never.*"

Straightening his shoulders, Chet looked first at Rocky, who was listening open-mouthed, and then out to the perimeters of the cavern. "Maybe we can think of something else," he said.

She pulled him back to face her. "It's no time to turn gallant. I want to get out of here as much as you do, and it's the only chance I can think of."

"Yeah. Goddammit, it *is* the only chance." In a fit of anger, he yanked at the chain on his leg and felt it burn across his hand. "We ought to get ready."

Avon nodded. "The lieutenant might show up at any time now."

Chet dropped the chain and put both hands on her wrists, lifting them. He looked between her outstretched arms at the mature sixer body. The skirt was unsealed at the waist and torn at the thighs and molded to her full hips. The ripped blouse hung in remnants off her shoulders, and showed the bruised swell of cleavage. She was nothing like Juell, but she was beautiful. Even now, the sight of her gave him a fever of lust . . . He didn't want to think about it.

"All right," he said in ashen tones. "Take off your clothes."

18.
The Nothing Lieutenant

For a long while they lay there naked, waiting to hear the approaching footsteps in the tunnel. Side by side, they were separated not only by the narrow, polite space between their bodies, but by a preoccupation with things to come. Call it *rape*, Chet thought. Cold and calculated and full of the wrong emotions; but he had no doubts as to the necessity.

Before the footsteps, he heard the lieutenant's laserod striking against the side of the narrow corridor. Then the boots, stamping unrhythmically, crushing pebbles, kicking stones . . . Chet drew a silent breath. From here on it was do or die, and he wouldn't give odds either way.

The sound of boots grew louder.

Chet rose up on an elbow and turned over on top of Avon. She closed her eyes. Her face was completely blank. At the start she put her arms limply around his back and let her legs lay flat; and then, as if she suddenly remembered her lines or turned on a switch, she began moving in a reasonable simulation of the real thing; arms squeezing, knees up, shoulders twisting. Chet put his lips on her mouth and a hand on her breast. But his teeth were set tightly; he could ill afford to let his plans get lost in a careless surge of desire.

"Earthman!" A guttural voice exploded the silence and boomed from the cavern walls.

The shout seemed to come from the distance of the

archway that was the entrance to the open area. Stubbornly, Chet made no change in movement or position, except to increase the tempo of his attack on Avon. Their hips rolled together in the dirt. His mouth pressed harder on hers. His hands ravished her body. But his thoughts were keenly tuned to every step of the boots.

"*Earthman!*" Closer.

Avon opened her eyes. Chet watched her face for clues to the boiling scene behind him.

"*McCoy!*" From right above now and more personal.

Avon screamed. "Look out, Chet! He's—"

Chet pulled away and dove to the side. The chain on his leg yanked him back. He fell, and winced, and looked up. He didn't like what he saw—the barrel of the down-turned blaster and the twisted features of the raging lieutenant—but he knew that up to that point his plan had worked, perhaps too well. The lieutenant was a green-eyed fiend, his soul in the grip of jealous anger, and intent on destruction.

The Rock was creeping around the pillar; catlike, quick and sure and steady. He carried his chain in one hand so that it wouldn't scrape on the ground. His other hand was partly open, his strong fingers poised in the form of a claw.

The lieutenant spat something in eighter gibberish and his knuckles grew white on the blaster.

"Now!" Chet yelled.

He twisted away as Rocky lunged for the gun hand. The blaster went off and tore up the ground next to Chet's ear, and he could still feel the heat as Rocky slashed at the lieutenant's hand to prevent another blast. The gun fell. Chet sprang for it. The lieutenant roared like a resurrected Earth tiger and swung at Rocky with both fists clasped together. The Rock went down. Chet wrapped the fingers of his right hand around the blaster. The lieutenant whirled and saw him and stepped backward. Rocky was up again, like a mastiff on a leash, straining to get at him. Chet struggled up to an elbow and raised the blaster. The lieutenant, defending himself, whipped the laserod from his belt and lifted it like a rifle; but Chet squeezed the blaster first.

The shot of flame tore off one shoulder and blackened an upper portion of the lieutenant's chest. For a moment he straightened and stiffened, statuesquely frozen with the brandished laserod. His eyes were dark and wide. His mouth opened slowly, then clenched with the spasm that ripped through his body, and he toppled backward.

Too far, Chet thought instantly.

He slammed his hands on the hard ground. "The key card!" he said.

Avon's face clouded. Chet watched her mentally measure the distance to the fallen lieutenant. He watched her glance around the cave for a tool. He watched her look back at him, almost disbelievingly.

She said, "We can't reach him."

That brought Rocky up to date, and his head swiveled to the same places. "How are we gonna get unlocked now, huh?"

Chet's voice was cold and deliberate.

"If we don't get the key card," he said, "our lives are over. He may be only a nothing lieutenant, but his absence won't go unnoticed for long. They'll be coming in here looking for him, and there are only a few blasts left in this gun."

He pulled the unbreakable chain taut from the pillar to his ankle, and stretched out prone on the ground. It made him realize that he was still naked, but he went on with it, putting rubber in every bone, throwing his arms forward until his shoulders protested and refused to give further, and the chain cut a ridge in his leg. He came a lot closer than he had estimated, and that made it even more infuriating. There was less than a handful of space between his reaching fingers and the toe of the lieutenant's boot.

It could have been a space league or a millimeter, for all the difference it made. He was stretched to the maximum, and he was the tallest and the closest of the three prisoners. His arms and legs ached. There was dirt in his mouth. And, he observed cheerlessly, there was nothing around the pillar that could be used to cross the chasm.

He eased back.

The chain had been threaded through his pants leg. Unthreading it, he remaneuvered into his clothes and sealed his shirt. Avon was dressed again, too, however incompletely.

Rested, Chet went out for the lieutenant again. All the way until the chain tightened. All the way until his stomach muscles started to tear. All the way until his arms felt numb. All the way, and no farther. He dug his fingers into the ground.

"It can't be done," he said from that position. "There's no way in space for us to get that key card." He closed his eyes and tried to think. There had to be a way.

"I can get it for you," said a voice from across the cave.

Chet raised his head. Even when he saw her standing in the archway, he couldn't believe that she had spoken or that she was there at all. He looked mistily at the small figure, the dark black hair in the white headband, the wicked eyes; and he knew that, believe it or not, it was her.

"Juell," he murmured.

She came and knelt beside him.

"Sweetie, it wasn't supposed to be like this. He told me—Abraxas told me himself—that he'd find passage for you to another SunStop. He didn't tell me about this. I didn't know, sweetie . . . I didn't know."

"It's all right, honey," Chet said. "Get me the key card for these chains."

"I will. Abraxas is as bad as Pawk Ludinder. Now he tells me that he has to kill you. I won't let him. I love you, Chet."

Chet moved back from his flat outstretched position and rubbed his arms. "Does anyone know you came in here?"

"No, I made sure," Juell replied. "Sweetie, will you take me with you?"

"I'll take you anywhere. Get the key card."

"Where is it?"

"In *his* pocket–I hope."

Juell wrinkled her nose. "I don't like to touch him."

"Get it, honey," Chet implored her. "Hurry. Someone might stroll in here at any minute."

Juell didn't think so.

"There aren't many of them around," she explained. "At last they've gone to win the war, after a year of skirmishes and recruiting. Tonight they started the big attack. Abraxas is here with a few officers and men. All the others are gone, to take Decatur, to throw out Ludinder. And they'll probably do it. But you, sweetie . . . you and me . . . we'll be far away and not care about it."

"Then let's go," Chet said, more brightly. "Get the goddamn card."

Juell moved gingerly to the lieutenant's body and began searching through the remains of his jacket.

"I think he's still alive," she said.

"He can't last long," Chet replied. "Let him suffer."

In no more than a minute she found the key card in the back pocket of the pants, and she tossed it to Chet. He turned, sitting up, and went to work on the chain.

The lock clicked open.

He threw off the du-metal cuff and massaged his

ankle. Then he let Avon loose. Then he threw the card to Rocky.

As he was helping Avon get to her feet, he turned to give his thanks to Juell for her timely reappearance.

"Well, you really got here in—*look out!*"

He leaped to shove her out of the way, and he was still in midair when he saw it happen.

The lieutenant, spilling blood from his chest and his empty arm socket, had risen to his knees with his laserod in his remaining hand. And that hand, when Chet first saw it, was swinging for Juell; and as he watched it, as he dove to prevent it, he saw the concentrated razor edge of light touch Juell's tiny waist a split second after it left the open end of the laserod—a silent, irretrievable beam!

He saw it but he couldn't accept it. A spinning black cloud wiped it away and whirled him into shock, befogging his mind, his sight, and every horrified nerve in his body; a tornado of Jupiter that came in and through him, moving his hands and feet with its rampageous power, burning in his chest, and then erupting from his mouth in a rabid roar. And through the inner storm he spun in its wind and darkness; no weight, no trajectory, no thought, and only a vague notion of a series of perpetual actions: lifting and roaring and hitting, and roaring and hitting, and hitting . . .

Someone was banging at his face.

"Dammit, Chet, quit it already." It was Rocky's voice trying to penetrate. "You musta mashed every bone he had. It ain't gonna do no good no more. He's dead, dammit. Quit it."

The blue light of the cavern came into Chet's eyes. The first thing his senses registered was the worried look on Rocky's face. Chet pushed him aside.

Beyond him, Avon had her arms wrapped weakly around the center pillar. Her face was white. She was vomiting.

The lieutenant was crumpled at the base of the craggy wall. He was a pulp of torn flesh and crushed bones. He was twisted and bent and dead. He was from boot to boot a nothing lieutenant, just as Juell had always said.

Juell.

Chet forced his eyes to her. Beautiful Juell. Her dreams and her courage and her love for ancient Earth music. All there, in sudden and violent death. Perhaps even more violent to the onlooker. Chet lowered his head and covered his eyes with both hands, but the image went on burning deep, permanent scars in his mind.

She was cut in half by the laser.

Cut in half.

19.
The Abraxas Search

Chet's eyes skipped over the living and the dead, and focused with some leftover traces of temporary insanity on the blaster that had dropped to the ground near the pile of discarded chains. He stepped to it, bent to it, grasped it; and he stood again, unsteadily at first, then becoming straight and solid as he read the meter that was embedded in the blaster's grip.

"A lot of shots left," he said. The weapon weighed lightly and purposefully in his hand. "At least one of them has to be for Abraxas."

"Maybe you'd better let me use it," said Rocky concernedly.

"Why?"

"Huh?"

"Why should *you* use the blaster?"

"Well . . . I'm a better shot," the Rock replied, but Chet could tell that he wasn't worried about degrees of marksmanship as much as he was remembering the man who'd gone berserk a few minutes ago.

Chet himself had no very clear idea of his own ability to function. If someone at that point had asked him to quote the odds on a simple freefall, the reply would have been a blank stare, for his head was soaked to the brim with uncool designs on the life of Abraxas, a Styman he had never even seen.

"Get your own gun," he said. "This one has an appointment with Abraxas's tonsils, and so do I. It's too goddamn late, but better than tomorrow and better than never. C'mon." He took a stride toward the corridor that had brought him into that part of the cavern, long ago today. "C'mon, we've got a lot of things to do. It's now—*now*—that we put this damn house in order!"

The dank cold smell of the air in the tunnel was a distinct variation to the surface atmosphere. So was the torchlight effect of the overused power cells. Chet tripped over a rock, marched a short distance down several devious passageways, then halted to get his bearings. He made his choice of direction, and went on.

His companions followed close behind him as they entered a fairly narrow underground corridor. Their footsteps rang hollowly in the confined space. Chet tucked the blaster in his belt so that he could have both hands free.

The passage led steeply downward and then leveled off. Chet had counted the steps on his way in; after twenty more paces he turned sharply, and the passage widened the way he seemed to remember it. Thirty paces beyond the turn he stopped again, and there was a brief delay while he and Rocky conferred about alternative openings in the underground maze. They continued maneuvers for another ten minutes and were finally rewarded with the sight they had been aiming for, the triangular main entrance to the cave, leading out to the crater.

From his vantage point Chet could see the backs of two rebels who were posted outside. But that was not the way he was going.

He took a step back to Avon.

"How do I find Abraxas?" he asked in a whisper. "Where did you talk to him at?"

She looked all around before she pointed. "Back through there, I think," she said, indicating one of the other passageways. "It's sort of a room . . ."

Chet started for it immediately. The others came

with him. They all quieted their footsteps now that they were in a more inhabited part of the cave.

The tunnel was a short span that ended bluntly. In front of Chet was a natural arch that probably led into another open area, but he couldn't tell for sure because it was covered by a drape of green cloth which was the only sign of privacy he had come across anywhere in the caverns.

"It has to be the royal suite," he said, and got a confirming nod from Avon. He took the blaster out of his belt. "If you two will excuse me for a while, I've got to see about burning the nose off of a Styman's head."

"I'm going with you," Rocky insisted.

"Behind me, then."

"OK. If you lemme have the blaster, I ain't gonna miss."

Chet shook his head. "If I miss, all the better. I'll do it with my bare hands."

"Yeah, but–"

"Rocky, do I look like I'm raving . . . or shaking . . . or blind?"

"No, but–"

"But *nothing*," Chet said sharply. "Let's go in."

With the blaster raised and ready to fire, he pushed aside the drape.

He seemed to be looking into a spacious underground cellar. Although it was furnished more like a room than any other part of the cave layout, it still was pervaded by a damp basement chill that was beyond the long reach of outdoor SunStop weather, and the non-solar light had the artificial glow of a burial tomb. A large eighter flag–but green, and of a different design than the government's–hung on the wall facing him, above a long table or desk on top of which sat a portable computer and a map generator. Behind the table were two chairs. On the left side of the table was a small bed, more like a cot.

Half-hidden under the cot were Chet's two suitcases. He hoped they were still full of the money; just as he hoped at the first instant that one of the two men in the room was Abraxas.

One of the men was lying on the cot and the other was sprawled in a chair. Both of them were half-asleep. From their attitudes and statures and unkempt outfits it was obvious after a moment's study, to Chet's extreme disappointment, that neither of them was the leader he was looking for. He leveled the blaster.

"Rise and shine, rebels," he said. "You're missing all the fun."

They both twisted their necks and came suddenly alert. The man on the cot let out a bronchial wheeze, but the man in the chair grabbed for the laserod which was lying across his lap. Steadily, Chet put both hands on the blaster and fired it. The man, the chair, and the laserod turned black together; the man clutched his chest and died soundlessly. It bothered Chet less than his previous killings . . . He seemed to be getting the knack.

The other man was not as foolish. A laserod was propped against the edge of the cot, but he was wise and cautious enough to ignore it. He wheezed again.

"Stand up," Chet told him.

The man, who was fairly fat and had a gray beard, replied miserably under his breath.

"Up, *up*," Chet said more loudly, and used his hands to stress the point. As the man rose from the cot, Chet walked over to him and touched the tip of the blaster to the edge of his beard. "Where's Abraxas?"

The man's eyes popped. "I'm *not* Abraxas!"

"I know," Chet said. "Where is he?"

Pointing to himself, the man shook his head wildly. "Not me, not me!"

"Goddammit, where is he? Abraxas. Where's that space-sucker Abraxas?"

A wary gleam of understanding came onto the man's frightened face. Mumbling, he waved a hand toward an infinite place behind Chet. "Out in the crater," he said finally.

Chet half-turned, then turned back.

"Outside, is he? Well, we need some of the wonder-planet's fresh air ourselves. But you, pal—," he stared grimly at the fat man, "—have to stay where you are."

He put his left hand on the man's shoulder and wheeled him around; then with a shove sent him stumbling over to Rocky. The Rock, who seemed pleased to get into the action, wound up from his knees with a rising uppercut that snapped back the man's head and left him unconscious.

Rubbing his fist, Rocky looked down at his handiwork. His grin indicated that he'd found the job more to his liking, that *that* was the way things were done on Wiggen. To continue the homebred process, he knelt to go through the man's pockets, but, finding no boozer pills nor anything of similar value, he stood again and gave the body a kick. Then, throwing off the disdain, he walked over to the cot and took possession of the laserod.

"OK," he said to Chet and Avon. "What do we do now, huh?"

Chet had been working on the answer to that question.

He said, "I've made up my mind. Since neither of these eighter heroes resembles a Sty god, our business is as unfinished as it was before. Abraxas is outside somewhere. So is the road home. But first things first, and that's Abraxas. Let's take the weapons and the bags of money, and go out of the cave and into the crater."

"There ain't much cover out there," Rocky warned.

"Don't worry, I don't want to die young," Chet replied. "But Juell said that most of the rebels were fighting in Decatur, and that there was only a skeleton force left behind. If it's still dark, and it must be, we should be able to sneak through them. Anyway, where's the choice?"

"Maybe we could find a different way outa the cave."

"And get lost forever in these goddamn tunnels. No, thanks." Chet stored the blaster in his belt. "Besides, I still need to meet up with Abraxas. Let's go. Avon, can you handle the small suitcase?"

"Hell, yes," she said.

"Good. Rocky, you take the big one."

As Chet gave the last instruction, he was moving rapidly to the archway; and when he got there he ripped down the green drape and went out. In his opinion, they had wasted too much time in the room, even though there were compensating factors such as the recovery of the money and the acquisition of a laserod—neither of those items would be worth very much if the delay cost them their chance at escape. They would soon find out.

At the other end of the short tunnel, Chet found himself once more in a position behind the two sentries that were stationed at the mouth of the cave. They were looking outward for trouble, and that was their salvation; for had they turned around they would have been shot down by a blaster and a laserod. Instead, they were felled by the butt ends of the weapons and would probably survive to sentry another day.

From there Chet peered out into the night. He could see shapes and figures, snatches of movement. Twenty or thirty of the rebels? He wasn't sure.

Avon came alongside.

"Over there, Chet. The jitters! If we run for it . . ."

He glanced at the row of vehicles, then back at the shadowy figures wandering around the slope of the crater—one of those figures was Abraxas. He tried to think about it rationally. He was responsible for putting Avon here, and he owed her a way out, alive. But he also owed a lot, including his own life, to Juell; and on top of that, if Abraxas was really from the Sty System . . . It occurred to him that he had figured it out to a level of clarity that was beyond his first expectation.

"I can't leave yet, Avon," he said. "I've got to go out there and try to find Abraxas. Rocky—take Avon and the money, and get a jitter with as full a charge as you can find."

"No, I ain't going without you," Rocky answered firmly. "I can get Abraxas, too. We'll have a better chance."

It was a good offer; it was just one that Chet couldn't accept.

He said, "We can't leave Avon alone. Listen, Rocky, we need one of us for each job. *Yours* is to get Avon out of here. Hold the jitter for me as long as you can, and I'll try to make it back. But—," Chet made sure that Rocky could see his face, and made the order sound like it had no room for rebuttal, "—take off when you have to. As soon as there's any sign of trouble. Do you understand?"

The Rock sniffed. "God . . . damn."

There was sure to be further argument, Chet thought, as long as he stayed to hear it. They were his friends, and that's what they'd do. He touched a hand to the blaster to be certain it was still in his belt. The hard feel of it gave him some confidence. He turned quickly and slipped away.

Chet walked quietly and evenly through the midst of the scattered renegades who seemed like background extras for his own private holoshow. At times he came so close to one that he could have reached out and touched him, had he wanted to. But he was looking for a man who was tall and unique. He was looking for a Styman in a uniform of green du-cloth. Face after face, rebel after rebel, but no one fit; and

Chet changed places, searching for the one he had to destroy.

He kept on walking. How he managed, he wasn't sure; but he kept on. His steps unchanged, he tried to maintain the ordinary outward appearance that had protected him so far, doing nothing that would single him out in the darkness. With that anonymity, he worked his way over the slope of the crater in a gradual curve that would eventually take him back where he started. But as he headed onto the return path, he was abruptly blinded by a ray of light.

"Who are you?" a crackly voice demanded to know.

Chet grabbed for the blaster and fell flat to the ground.

In the few seconds that he was under the splash of light, he was able to see the face of the man who held the torch. The face was wrinkled, old, and toothless. The expression, however, had a ghoulish ferocity that matched the long-bladed knife in the man's hand, a knife that glinted less than a single meter from Chet's throat. Quickly, the torch in the man's other hand swung down, and Chet was blinded again by the light; but he had seen enough. He raised his blaster to the source of the light and matched it with an exploding ball of flame.

The scream came after the sound of the shot, and turned the crater into a hotbed of alert rebel fighters.

Chet rose to a crouch.

He could no longer pose as a compatriot in the darkness. They knew where he was, and a disorganized squad of them was already running to the spot. He fired a blast to break them up, and in turn a pair of laser beams crossed closely above his head. He got up and ran.

Full speed, he arrived at the mouth of the cave and knelt there, breathing hard, feeling a numbness in his legs. He turned the blaster outward and waited for the rebels to catch up. At that point he knew he couldn't win; he would die. His hope was that somewhere in the approaching group he could find and kill Abraxas. But as they closed in, even that last hope faded. In the night, in the mass of shadows, all of the attackers were identical. He could probably cut a few of them down . . . But without Abraxas, it was a cheap way to sell his life.

He took a pot shot that disintegrated a boulder and did no further damage. He didn't care. He fired again, haphazardly. It didn't matter to him where the blasts went now. The gamble was already lost. He couldn't escape; he couldn't kill Abraxas. All that was left on this eighter world was to play out the game, and he was fast tiring of the game.

He heard tires squeal, almost on top of him.

"Chet, c'mon!" Rocky was leaning out of the jitter, grabbing for his arm.

20.
A Pack of Jitters

Suddenly the game was new; vibrantly fresh and different.

Chet leaped for the back seat of the jitter, one arm linked with Rocky's and the other arm waving the blaster. Laser beams and blastfire followed him.

"Move it!"

"Yeah, man," snorted the Rock. The jitter spun around one-hundred-eighty degrees like a top.

The quick turn knocked Chet down in the seat. Climbing up again, he faced back to the cave where he'd been, and managed to stay there while Rocky tore over the dirt road toward the ridge of the crater. It was just starting to get light. Fortunately, the first sun was rising to the left ahead of them and shining back into the rebels' eyes.

"They're going for the other jitters," Chet reported. "Keep your foot on the floor and don't worry about bumps. Just *go*."

Rocky struggled with the steering. "Where, huh?"

"Out of the crater. Anywhere." Briefly, Chet glanced up front to where Avon and the Rock were sitting, then looked beyond them up the slope. Where was a place for the three of them on this planet? he wondered. *Nowhere*. He kept his voice loud so Rocky could hear him. "Can you find your way back to Matann? To where you left the pod?"

"Hey, that's right, Chet. I bet the damn pod's still

sitting there. What a deal, huh? We can jump on and scram."

"First we have to get there," Chet said. He stayed low, looking over the back of the seat. They were being chased by three jitter-loads of rebels. Each jitter was packed like a school bus, and every dirty kid had the face of a super-zealous killer.

"Getting there ain't going to be easy," Rocky was saying. "This crummy thing is slowing down."

Chet turned to him. "Slowing down?"

"I can't help it." Cursing, Rocky shook the wheel and stamped his foot up and down on the go-pedal. Next to him, Avon offered a share of her SunStop experience.

"It's running out of the stored charge," she said. "But it's light enough now—you can switch to direct sun."

"How do I do that, huh?"

Avon did it for him, touching a stud on the dash. The jitter came almost to a stop during the switch-over; then burst forward faster than ever. Rocky gave her a grateful grin.

"Good thing you're here, doll. I don't know nothing about driving these foreign cars."

"You're doing all right," she said.

"Yeah, huh? How about that?"

Chet rapped him on the shoulder. "But do it faster."

"Faster? Stick it up your tubes! What do you think this is—a soarer?"

"We'll never make it to the pod," Chet said, "if we don't put some distance between us and them."

"So shoot 'em or something."

"I can't hold this blaster steady enough. Let me try the laserod."

The weapon was bouncing in the front seat; Rocky caught it and handed it back. Chet took aim midway up the front of the first jitter, a point that allowed the most margin for error, and he missed. The ride was too bumpy to do better. He tried again and, just as he fired, his own jitter went up over the top of the crater ridge and leveled out, sending the laser beam wildly into the cloudless blue sky.

But they were on their way to the main road.

Once there, Avon picked up on the road signs and handled directions. Rocky was sweating, a rare condition in the SunStops and not caused by heat or sunshine. The sunshine, however, was filtering through the solar panel and providing all the speed that the road and driver could handle. The problem was, the other jitters had the same sun.

It worried Chet that the pursuing rebels were still too close, although the separation was perhaps a few meters more than it had been on the way up the crater. Even if his own jitter was the first to reach the pod, how would they get time to get aboard and take off? As soon as they stopped the jitter . . . Yet where else was there to go? Both Ludinder and Abraxas now had cause to kill them on sight. Run from one and meet the other. It had to be the pod.

Ninety-to-one, and ties lose.

They drove into the city of Matann. Chet noted that there were no visible signs of combat. The battle, he assumed, was at the moment confined to Decatur; with the exception of these four jitters that were tearing silently and swiftly through the streets.

He sat around in the seat.

"Do you know where you're going?"

Rocky nodded vigorously. "Yeah, now I got it down pat. That's the beach right at the end of this street. The pod's on the beach."

"Drive onto the beach," Chet said. "Get as close to the pod as you can."

"I'll park in the tubes," Rocky assured him.

But the assurances fell flat a minute later, after Rocky had driven off the road and plowed through the white sand, parallel to the line of crystal clear foam that was breaking from the sea. Ahead of them, in the sunlight, were *two* structures and a lot of men.

Chet leaned forward with an arm on the front seat. He could see the men well enough to identify their eighter uniforms; there was no mistaking the bright red loops on their shoulder patches. Some of the men were on the beach, some were going into the pod . . . It was evident that the getaway ship had been discovered and taken over by Ludinder's forces.

Rocky didn't slow down. "Look at that!"

"Who the hell are they?" Avon asked.

"Looks like the government troops," Chet said. "That's one of their soarers sitting next to the pod."

"Damn cops," said the Rock. "Can't get away from them nowhere. What do you want me to do now, huh?"

Chet pointed straight ahead.

"Keep going! Abraxas's men are on the beach right behind us. We can't turn back."

"We can't go straight, neither. Them jokers'll throw us in the jug for stealing the pod."

"Don't worry about *that,*" Chet told him quickly. "They're more likely to shoot first—and last. But keep going. Not *to* them. Past them. Barrel right past them."

No sooner did the words come out than Rocky took care of the action, steering the jitter with uneven control and passing close by the perimeter of troops, leaving a number of them astounded and covered with showers of sand. But, looking back as they sped on down the beach, Chet found no amusement in it, for the forces on his neck were now doubled and the slim chances he had figured on when they started for the pod were—

"It ain't gonna do no good!" Rocky yelled suddenly. He shoved hard on the brakes and slid in the sand to a stop, turning their jitter sideways.

As Chet came around, he caught the whole panorama of the high wall that loomed up in front of them. It began far to the left, went straight past the jitter, and continued unbroken to the edge of the water . . . and from there a deck was built out over the sea. It appeared to be the side wall of one of the old casino–hotels, now boarded up and abandoned until such time as some future rebellion changed the way things were. But the way things were now, it was directly in the path of their only escape route. Driving, walking, or climbing, there was no visible way to go around it, over it, or through it. It was solidly there to stay. And so, Chet thought, were they.

"Get out and down," he said, pushing Avon ahead of him.

They crouched behind the jitter with the building at their backs. Rocky raised his blaster over the top of the hood, and Avon peered cautiously over the seats in the middle. At the rear end of the vehicle Chet lifted the laserod—he still did not feel accustomed to it and would have preferred another blaster—and sighted down the sandy terrain that now glistened in second sunrise.

A loud shot turned a piece of the beach black, near the base of the pod. One of Ludinder's men melted into it.

"Stay down," Chet said. "Looks like we got here just in time for the war."

From his spot he had a good view. The government troops, who at first might have considered going after the single jitter that had sped past them, were diverted completely and quickly by the three jitters full of rebels that followed. As the enemies recognized each other . . .

The rebels started shooting while they were still on the approach. The troops responded immediately, returning the fire, and many of them ran toward their soarer for cover and better weapons. Meanwhile, the jitters stopped in a protective semicircle, letting the rebels spill out and disperse. About half of the rebel group, maybe less, stayed behind the jitters. They fired a heavy barrage of beams and blasts that allowed the other half to peel off and attack the soarer. After that the beach was ablaze with fighting, with bodies in uniforms and bodies in rags falling onto the sand, full of holes or disintegrating.

It stopped as suddenly as it began.

Chet let out a deep breath. The battle was over. It had lasted no more than fifteen minutes. It had demonstrated the enthusiasm and fighting power of Abraxas's insurgents. It had proved that government troops are lousy shots. If the scene on the beach was any model of the real war in Decatur, or of future infiltrations from the Sty System, then Ludinder and this section of the galaxy was in serious trouble. Ludinder deserved it, but the rest of the wonderplanets . . . Chet wasn't sure how much credit to give to the Stys for training and leadership, but he knew this much: if a soarer full of government troops had been defeated so easily, what chance could there be for a couple of Earth bookies and a sixer maiden?

And they had not been forgotten. As Chet watched, the rebels regrouped and changed directions.

"We're next," he said soberly. "Looks like there's ten or fifteen of them left out there. We have a laserod and a blaster, both of which have been used a lot."

Rocky checked the meter on his blaster and grimaced.

"And we ain't got no spare charges."

"Even if we did," Avon said between them, "there's only three of us."

"I don't think there's any way . . ." Chet summed up. He narrowed his eyes and spat over the top of the jitter. "But, goddammit, let's not make it easy for them."

At the front, Rocky came up and took aim with him.

"I'm gonna—" The first blast cut off the Rock's words.

The second blast scorched the middle section of the jitter and caused Avon to huddle on the ground. Then a narrow laser-beam traveled closely over their heads. Others came at different heights from different angles as the intensity increased beyond count. The jitter shook with laser hits; it was getting red hot and Chet saw pieces of it tear loose and go flying. The beach around them was becoming a map of dark blotches. Then the building in back of them burst into flame.

Within the holocaust, Chet nodded to Rocky, and they fired a brief volley in return. And that's the way it would be, Chet thought. A burst now and then to keep the rebels from full attack. Until the two weapons were used up.

"Stupid starshit!" Rocky was snorting. He had his teeth clenched and was staring hatefully at the blaster in his hand. "I ain't hardly done nothing, and this damn thing is almost uncharged."

"So's mine," Chet said, and he felt a colder kind of emptiness in the center of his stomach.

He brought in the laserod and checked it. Maybe two shots. He checked it again. *Two shots.* From across the beach they were coming in tens, and he had two useless shots in his stockpile. *Sonuvabitch.* He slammed the butt end of the laserod against the jitter. He opened and closed his hands to relax his fingers, then leaned forward again with the weapon, watching every move of his attackers.

They were getting bolder at the lack of resistance. Some of them had their heads raised; some were venturing out in front of their jitters.

"Give 'em a blast!" Chet bellowed, and Rocky started to shoot.

This time the Rock had open targets. Four bursts

came from his blaster, and three men dropped. The others fell back to their protected positions.

Chet felt a hand on his shoulder.

"That's all, buddy," said Rocky. "I've run dry."

"Well, there's a couple left in here," Chet replied with all the calmness he could manage. "We'll save them for the last ditch and then . . ."

A thought came into his mind that made him forget every word he'd just said. He strained his eyes to see the line of rebel vehicles. Somewhere about dead center a man's face was lifted above the jitter. The face turned to the left, then to the right, shouting commands in a strong voice. An arm, *in a bright green sleeve*, came up to emphasize the orders. The arm interested Chet for only a moment, then he went back to studying the face. Square and perfectly cut. Thick brows and straight black hair. Godlike. Or like the legendary images of the pioneers of space . . . only . . . only . . . a Sty!

Abraxas.

Chet's stupefied gaze hung on the image. It was impossible for him to put together a rational thought. His feud with Abraxas was something beyond the potential threat to the looping SunStops, even above the toppling of universal governments. It was a personal, gnawing thing. Now that he faced the Styman—now that he found the man he'd been searching for—all he could consider was the murder of Juell and the rape of Avon and everything that had been done to him. All he could feel was his hand on the laserod.

He stood without ever getting to the rational thought.

"Abraxas!" he yelled across the beach. "Stand up, you space-sucker!"

The shooting stopped in an uncalled truce.

"Abraxas . . .!" Chet went on shouting it until far off in front of him the figure started to rise from behind the jitter. The Sty god. Standing.

Chet didn't wait.

He aimed with a precision he'd never possessed, and touched the switch.

The first rope of laser light hit the jitter, harmlessly. The second beam traveled true and hit Abraxas in the chest, and Chet saw him stagger back from the blow. There was no third shot. The laserod was empty. No matter, Chet thought, it had been a damn good last fight.

What the hell—?

The realization came to him slowly, perhaps because at first he rejected its possibility. But when it came to him, it ripped his nerves. Instinctively, he lifted the laserod again and banged at the switch, pleading for more juice, clicking and clicking on the used-up chamber; until at last he took the weapon by the barrel and hurled it with all his strength at the incredible phantom.

Abraxus was still standing. Not bent and not bleeding, his arm was raised up in a new set of orders, and the rebels started firing again.

A sharp piece of the jitter caromed off Chet's shoulder and knocked him to the ground. Rocky and Avon came close to examine him.

"It ain't much," the Rock said comfortingly.

Chet didn't care about it.

"I didn't miss him," he said between his teeth. "Rocky, I know I didn't miss him. I *saw* him get hit."

"Yeah, I seen it, too," was the reply. "But I seen it like that before. The beam makes the guy jump like one of my wellsprings on Wiggen, but it don't hurt him none. Betcha a grand that the joker's wearing some kind of armor or something. A laser-proof jacket, huh?"

"So the goddamn joke's on me," Chet said.

Avon was crying. "Chet . . ."

"Leave me alone. I don't know what else to do.

We've lost this game all the way around." He moved away from her. "Goddammit, sometimes you lose."

Rocky was up at the jitter.

"They're coming now!" he warned.

Chet struggled up beside him. His left shoulder was throbbing. His eyes were tired and his head ached from all the hurried and useless efforts. But the rebels were advancing. All of them, a cautious step at a time through the sand. Chet counted: Abraxas and his last seven men, together in front of their vehicles, moving up on the careful assumption that all opposing weapons were discarded. In another minute the rebels would be shooting again. One well-put blast or three point-blank laser beams was all they would need.

Chet's mind continued to race futilely, automatically recalculating the odds and checking off the time in eighter increments. *What else was there?* They couldn't even try to run for it with the high flaming wall behind them. His tired gaze went to the insides of the scorched jitter, looking for any and all weapons that could help him fight it out to the end. *Anything,* he pleaded silently. A crowbar, a knife, a length of pipe—anything. His eyes glazed over. There was nothing. There were only the same two suitcases of money that had always been the burden on his back.

Out on the sea the two suns were coming together.

Abraxas's eyes were close enough to reflect an alien brightness enhanced by the taste of victory. His uniform was green and unsoiled. His jackboots were kicking up the beach.

The rebels were halfway home.

Chet sank down and sat with his back against the jitter. He was extremely tired. He'd been fighting, he remembered, ever since the night he was kidnapped from his room at the Towers. The lottery . . . Juell . . . the android . . . and after he cleaned out Ludinder's vault, everything had come to a peak and stayed there. He was tired of it all. What good did any of it do?

A past thought scrambled back again and fired every nerve in his body. He bolted straight up.

"When I cleaned out Ludinder's vault," he said, and raised it to a shout. "When I . . . cleaned out . . . the vault!"

He got puzzled glances from Rocky and Avon.

"I'm not crazy," he went on. "Avon, don't you . . . Rocky, get the small suitcase."

The Rock spread his hands. "Hell, Chet. A payoff ain't going to do it. They get all the money anyway as soon as they blast us."

"Ah, but who's going to blast *who?*" Chet demanded. "Get the damn bag!"

Rocky lunged for the floor of the jeep and brought it out. Chet grabbed it from him. It was hot and burnt on the edges, but Chet tore it open and it was clean inside. Turning it over, he dumped it on the ground and dug his hands into the pile of eighter dollars. When his hands came out of the pile, they were loaded, literally.

Rocky's jaw dropped. "Blastpins!"

"And shipped to me directly from Abraxas," Chet explained. He was pleased with the irony of it. "I didn't know how to use them to blow open a vault, but for this . . . There are three of them. Avon, can you handle one?"

"Yes," she answered evilly, tossing back her hair. "Hell, yes."

"Then there's one for each of us." Chet handed them out and demonstrated. "Like this. When I tell you, pull out the ends and push them back together. When I tell you again, throw 'em." He looked out to the beach. The rebels, he noted, were very close and still cautious, but they were grouped together and Abraxas was right in the middle. Chet turned back quickly. "Okay, now."

In exactly ten seconds by his time implant Chet gave the next signal; and they drew back their arms and hurled the blastpins.

"Love it, you bastards!" Chet yelled as he watched his sail out toward Abraxas's jackboots. Then he yelled, "Down!" but the others were there ahead of him, waiting for him as he dropped to curl himself against the bottom of the jitter.

The blasts arrived one on top of the other; the sound came first, the monumental roar of explosives set free. Then everything seemed to be churning. The beach, the sky, the water, the jitter . . . all knuckling under to a man-made quake.

After which everything was very still.

Avon broke the spell. "Chet, your shoulder . . ."

"The hell with it," he said, and rose to his feet.

He looked around. A huge black hole was burned into the beach. There were no people anywhere. Only charred evidence of the carnage. Then he noticed something on the front seat of the jitter. He bent over to get a closer look, but he didn't touch it.

It was an arm. A full-muscled arm. The sleeve around it was ripped and shredded and seared, but some of the sharp pleat remained, and some of the original color and texture was there.

Green du-cloth.

If there were really any Stymen in the galaxy, there was one Sty less.

21.
Winners Take All

"Mmmm," she sighed. "It's *so* good to be civilized again."

"I'll go along with that," Chet said. They were on the couch high up in his spindle, revolving leisurely in the perfect twilight of SunStop 6, and he was selecting boozer pills from the wide-mouthed decanter on the coffee table. He turned away from them to look at her, from head to toe. "Still, there's something to be said for the caveman bit."

Avon reddened. "You're supposed to forget that."

"Nothing is ever forgotten," he told her.

At the center of the room the tube lit up and its door slid open.

"It's just like you figured," Rocky advised as he walked in. "The pod is gone. I went up and down where we left it, and there ain't even a trace. They took it away."

"Good," said Chet. "I want it to get back to its owner."

Rocky shrugged, unconcerned. He folded his arms. "Well, what do I do now, huh?" he wanted to know.

"Go away, pal." Chet handed Avon a blue pill and one that had red stripes. He smiled encouragingly.

"Huh?" asked the Rock.

"Go get us AmDrive reservations for . . . say, about next week."

"I don't got no money."

"Take a handful of the eighter dollars and get them exchanged."

"OK." Rocky opened the bag and took *two* handfuls. After all, sixer women had expensive tastes and it was going to be at least another week before he got back to Brauna. "See you later," he said, and left with a grin.

And Avon said, "What'll you do with the rest of it?"

Chet picked up the decanter and measured the level of boozers with one eye closed.

"Well," he said, "we can take them all now or save some for tomorrow. There are *some* things I don't mind postponing." He looked straight into her green eyes.

"I mean the rest of the money."

"The loot?" He took his eyes off her just long enough to see that the suitcases were still there. When he looked back, he had it solved. "As far as I know, I'm still running the eighter lottery; and as my last official act, I proclaim the winning ticket to be the one that Rocky bought in Matann." He snapped his fingers. "It's a good chunk for our trouble. And I'll leave some behind for you. Now, if that takes care of all of your questions—"

"Shhh," she said.

She twisted, reaching over the arm of the couch to turn up the volume of the beamer. The soft music and its surrealistic light-projections had turned into a rasping newstape.

". . . *and the fighting continues, spread throughout the outermost wonderplanet. Reports have been sketchy and unreliable, with both sides claiming victories. However, all Decatur beamer facilities are now in the hands of—*"

Chet clicked it off, climbing over Avon to do it. She looked up at him, wide-eyed.

"What the hell did you do that for?"

"Because without me and the Stys there," he said,

"who cares who wins?" He took the pills out of her hand and set them back on the table. He put his feet up on the cushions of the couch, and his lips close to hers. "All I care about right now, honey," he went on, "is you and the next feature freefall from the rings of Saturn. And I don't give too much of a damn about the freefall."